APRIL FOOLS

Diana Bettinson

Best Wishes

He is dead, my husband is dead,

A shot gun wound to the head

That's what the policeman said

Now I must learn to live without you

Being here to tell me what to do.

But who is that woman and child?

My steady husband, where you really wild?

Do I want to live in this house?

And carry on being a mouse?

Or can I now live a proper life

All be it not as your wife.

A challenge with each new day

Learning to find my own way.

Birthdays, anniversaries, Christmas, and New Year

The sadness the grief and devastating tears.

Without you controlling every move I made

There's freedom to break the rules you laid.

Doing some things I always liked to do

Instead of always deferring to you.

Now I can change the way I look and what I eat

Your exacting standards I don't have to meet.

You kept me isolated from my friends

Now all that has come to an end.

Thursday April 1st

It's a joke isn't it? An April fool's joke? I must say it isn't very funny if it's a bloody joke. They are telling me that you're dead, Harry. That can't be right.

That was Paula's first thought that awful morning, that someone was playing a horrible trick on her. The police had arrived on her doorstep at ten minutes past ten in the morning. There was a female uniformed police officer, an older male one and some other woman, they introduced as a Police Liaison Officer called Liz.

They asked Paula to sit down and the young woman police officer went to make tea. That worried her right away. They said that her husband Harry had been found early this morning by a man walking his dog. That he had been shot in the head and a shot gun had been found beside him.

That's about the time she stopped listening to them, her stomach was churning, and she felt sick and dizzy and could feel something rising in her. Hysteria.

How can you be dead, you are my husband? We have been together thirty two years and have hardly been apart in all that time. I think I was telling them that and they had to have made a mistake. It couldn't be you Harry. You made a vow never to leave me. You have been my life for all that time, my other half. Literally two parts of one whole. That's what you called us. I am watching myself, sitting there on the couch screaming, crying drowning in these terrible feelings.

The older officer spoke into his radio perhaps he was calling for a doctor.

'Mrs. Thompson, please drink some tea,' the young one said. I think that's when I threw the mug at her. They were still trying to talk to me but I didn't hear them, I had an awful rushing sound in my head and then tunnel vision. They asked if there was anyone who could be with me. I tried to tell them I wanted my husband but I couldn't get the words out. All I seemed to be able to manage was screaming. Then I think I fainted. Harry, where are you? I need you here.'

Friday 2nd April

Paula woke up and for the first few seconds she luxuriated in the comfort of her bed, then the realisation hit her that something really rather terrible had happened. She looked at the clock and saw it was again ten minutes past ten. How long had she slept? She didn't feel well, had she been drugged?

'Oh God, Harry,' Paula cried out.

'Good morning Paula, how are you feeling today?' Doctor Maples asked her. 'I expect you are feeling a bit groggy, I had to sedate you yesterday.'

'My husband is dead.'

'Yes, my dear. It was an awful shock for you and the police called me in to help. You have been sedated for a full day. It's Friday now. Molly and Sandi are downstairs, shall I call them, or do you feel able to get up?'

Still not fully able to take in what was being said to her Paula threw back the covers to see that she was still dressed in the night dress and fluffy matronly dressing gown that she was wearing yesterday when the police had given her the dreadful news.

'I'll get up now, thank you.'

'Right I'll leave you to it, if you feel at all shaky or anxious just give me a call and I can come out to see you again.'

'Thank you Doctor.'

Paula heard her daughters outside her room talking quietly with the Doctor and then she heard him leave the house and his car drive away, it was a few minutes before the girls came in.

Then the shock hit me again. Harry, you're dead. You really are dead. Never coming back. No more cuddles, no more silly jokes. Nothing. And the girls, they have lost their father. Their rock, forever a steadfast presence. That's not fair.'

'Do you want to get up Mum?' Molly asked as she entered the room. 'Doctor Maples said you would be alright now and that the sedation should have more or less worn off. '

'So, it's true, your Father has left us, he is really dead and gone.'

Both the girls had been crying, Paula could see their red rimmed eyes. They explained to Paula that they had stayed at the house all night to make sure she was not alone if she should wake up.

'I'll have a shower and be down in a few minutes, but first come and give me a cuddle both of you.'

Molly said, 'I think Liz is coming over this morning to see how you are.'

'Liz?'

'The liaison officer for the police.'

'Oh, her. Yes I remember now. I think I was quite rude to her. And I threw a cup at that nice young police girl.'

'I don't suppose she will worry too much about that, Mum.'

'Well, I need to get up and get clean, I feel really sticky and messy. How about a nice cup of tea? No, I will have coffee, I always preferred that in the morning.'

The girls went down to the kitchen while Paula took a shower and freshened up.

'I never knew Mum preferred coffee to tea, she always drinks tea.' She heard Sandi saying as she entered the Kitchen.

'Dad always likes tea. Liked tea. It seemed silly to make different drinks so I had tea with him.'

They sit for a while in silence as Paula nibbled at some toast. She tried to eat to please her daughters but didn't really want any food. She felt guilty at being able to eat when Harry could not.

'How did the children take it?' she asked. Stupid, the things you think of at times like this.

Sandi's twin girls are only four years old so don't really understand. Sandi said to her that when she told them they just accepted that Grandpa is not going to be around anymore. Dee and Zoe. Harry had never been keen on the names, but Paula liked them saying cute children should have cute names.

Molly's children are different though, Daniel, eleven, and Rachel, nine.

'They are devastated,' Molly told her.

Oh, poor children. My poor children. Harry, how could you leave us?

'I have to see him.' I said pulling my hand through my hair. I caught the girls glance at each other and then look down to the floor.

'What?' I demanded.

'I expect Liz will be able to arrange that,' Molly said. 'She did say that they would need a formal identification.'

'Will you be alright if we go home for a while Mum?' Sandi asked me.

'Yes darlings, of course. You have your families to see to. I will be fine here for a while.'

There was a knock at the kitchen door, Sandi opened it to find Liz waiting there. Sandi let her in and she introduced herself to Paula again.

'Good morning Mrs Thompson, you may not remember me, but I am Liz Stokely. Police liaison officer, we met briefly yesterday.'

'Yes, I think I am getting some memories back from yesterday. Hello again,' Paula answered her.

Molly and Sandi said their goodbyes and told Paula they would be back a bit later.'

When the girls had gone Liz sat down and asked Paula if she would be able to come to identify Harry.

She warned me that you do not look at your best, as she put it. I said I needed to see you anyway as I still could not believe that you had died, Harry. She said she could arrange it, for next Monday. Was there anything else she could do for me?

'You can tell me how my husband died,' I said.

'Well, I assume your daughters have told you about Harry's shotgun. It was propped up beside him and somehow he had his hand wrapped round it. It would seem that his thumb got caught in the trigger guard. It looks very much like he shot himself, Paula. What we have to do now is establish if he meant to do it or if it was a terrible accident.'

I feel numb, Harry. I know you would never do that on purpose. No. Not you.

'No, Harry had been looking forward to taking early retirement and not needing to going to work every day. He was such a workaholic, Harry never stopped. It's just not possible that he would do a thing like that.'

'Well, there will have to be a post-mortem to see if there were any underlying health issues. But so far the pathologist has ascertained that Harry died some twelve to fifteen hours before he was found.'

'So long? I thought he had gone out early in the morning.'

'The Inspector will need to see you, perhaps tomorrow? Just to ask a few questions to get things straight. And I will arrange for you to see Harry after the weekend. Will you be alright or do you want me to stay until one of your daughters can come back?'

'I will be alright thanks. I have some stuff to be getting on with.'

Liz gave me a card with her number on it and told me that she could come round any time I needed her to and she gave me some leaflets regarding counselling and one was called "What to do after a death".

Then she left me alone to grieve for you, Harry.

And to ponder on what happened. It was one of your guns, she said. I didn't hear you go to the gun cabinet. Was it locked now? Paula went to look. Yes it was locked, as she knew it would be but she couldn't find the key. The safe had lots of papers in but no gun cabinet key. Perhaps the inspector had it.

Oh Harry. What happened to us?

We met at the local hunt ball. I remember after about twenty minutes of conversation you told me that we would get married. You said it was love at first sight for you and you had noticed my nearly waist length blond hair you loved the way it waved about as I danced. It took me a little longer to fall in love with you. In fact Harry I wonder now if I ever did love you. We hardly knew each other. I could have been totally insane for all you knew. You could have been an axe-murderer or a wife beating drunk. But you insisted and we were married as soon as humanly possible, you said you couldn't wait. My parents were not best pleased but I thought I would take a chance on you. They did persuade us to wait for a while though. Nothing is forever, was one of my favourite sayings at the time. Such a happy go lucky girl, something else you said attracted you.

Besides you had a ready-made business and you had already bought this old house. When I first saw the house I was enchanted.

Even though it was somewhat run down Harry's house was beautiful. There was long drive way from the road between two fields, and then the house appeared round behind tall hedges. A seventeenth century long house. All beams and mullioned windows and painted a pale cream colour. There was a big lawn to the back but as the house stood the big main windows and doors to the garden gave the impression that in fact that would have been the front of the house. After the lawn there was a large pond with bull rushes around the edge and then the copse just a bit further on. The copse was actually the start of a very large wood which had public access.

The door off the drive way led directly to the kitchen. A big room and to the left was a long corridor off which was the dining room and then the lounge. Harry was living there in the kitchen which was big enough to be a dining room, lounge and still leaving space for a bed. He had also made a shower room at the end of the corridor next to a handy utility room. Paula could see the beauty of the house and could understand why Harry had bought it. The nearest neighbours were quite a long way off, at least two fields distant. When it was brought up to scratch with would be a very comfortable home.

Harry already had a business. A wholesale warehouse that supplied the local trades where Paula came to work so that they could spend as much time together as possible.

Harry looked at his friend Roger and said. 'Why in hell's name would I want to go to a Hunt Ball?'

'All work and no play does make Harry a very dull boy, my friend. It's for your own good. You are getting old before your time.'

'But a hunt ball?'

'Where else to find fit young ladies?'

'But they probably all look like horses and smell even worse.'

'They do wash and dress up for the ball, dear boy anyway I have a couple of tickets. If nothing else it's a good meal and cheap booze for the night.'

So Harry went along for what the though was going to be a boring evening with his oldest friend. He would rather have been sorting the vat returns out if he was brutally honest. Harry had a grand plan, he was fully intending to be rich. He already had one wholesale warehouse. It was doing good business and by undercutting all opposition he was gaining customers. He knew his was the cheapest wholesaler in the area, and he intended to be the only one.

He had also found a badly run-down house way out of town which he saw up for auction. He couldn't afford to buy it at the guide price but that is where Roger and a few other buddies came in handy. Harry had briefed them before the auction and a rumour was put about that the house, an old farm house was built on blighted land and was only fit to be demolished. It did not reach its guide price at the auction but Harry later bought it for half its value.

He congratulated himself on how clever this plan was. There was a lot of work to do to make it even habitable, but he knew he had his dream home and would never leave it. Who wanted to live in the town in a pokey flat when you could have all this? For now he had all he needed, and as time went on and he could afford it, he would renovate it. At least the roof was sound, no leaks. Sometimes at night when he lay in his bed in that one room and listened to the wind howling around the house he would visualise how the house would be when he had done some work to it.

When he was not at work in his warehouse he would be home working on the house. He understood Roger had concerns but this was all part of his grand plan. Fun could come later. When he was rich!

The two young men arrived at the hunt ball dressed in their black tie dinner suits and looked very smart. Harry, the taller of the two with his dark brown hair swept back and finely chiselled features looked particularly handsome. As he scanned the room he noticed a girl with very long blond hair. His deep brown eyes followed her as she found her seat and he thought himself lucky that he could continue to watch her from his own seat. He was aroused and just wanted to bury his face in her hair and breathe her in, when she had eaten her meal and got up to dance he couldn't take his eyes away. Thanks, Roger for bringing me here, he thought. You have just done me a bigger favour that even you know.

Harry knew he had met, or was about to introduce himself to his future wife. She was every bit as attractive when he spoke to her as she was to look at. Vivacious, intelligent, fun loving. She did talk about her horses, which bored Harry. He led the conversation in such a way that she had to ask questions to find out any information about him. A knack he had learned as a teenager. Information he wanted people to know but rather than just tell them and have them think he was self-centred, he would allow them to wheedle the information out of him. The evening went in a flash and far from being the boring night Harry thought it would be he really enjoyed himself.

Once married, Paula and Harry concentrated on building up the business and making a home for themselves in the lovely old house. From his humble beginning which was all on borrowed money, they now have warehouses all over the country. They both worked at the business and at making a home in the house. Both Paula and Harry became expert in buying and selling at work as well as building works on the house.

Molly's husband, Eric, came to work there and that's how they met. He learned the trade from Harry. Eric could be just as ruthless in the world of business as Harry, possibly even more so. This gave Harry confidence that he had chosen the right man for the job and the right husband for his daughter.

When Sandi met John, Harry persuaded him to join the business as well. That way he could keep a close eye on this budding relationship and this proved to be invaluable when John and Sandi married. He had his family just where he wanted them, close and under his control. Both these young men have proved themselves.

Paula had stopped work a few years back, which for Harry, by that time was a blessed relief. He was becoming very disenchanted with spending twenty four hours in Paula's company. When they were younger they could work and live together, they both agreed, unlike other couples they knew. But Harry felt that although he loved Paula, after all she was his wife and the mother of his children, she had become a bit boring and complacent.

She had no conversation, especially since she had retired. He needed the time he was at work as space to get away from her. She would talk about their lives before they met and even more boring stuff like horses.

We were together twenty four hours a day sometimes Harry, most of the time, in the early days. We sort of melted together into one unit. It's going to be hard without you, as if half of me had been ripped away.
Am I being selfish here? The girls are grieving for you as well. But right now I need to think about myself.

We worked hard to build the business. You always said you couldn't have done it if I hadn't been there with you all the way. Through two pregnancies. Bringing tiny babies into work, we both looked after them and made a really good business between us. We did everything together, cooking, child care, work, play. Oh, the play, we had some good times alone as well didn't we, Harry? We made love all night before the children arrived, and went to work looking like something out of a zombie film. Here, there and everywhere.

On the stairs, on the floor, in the shower, on the lawn, against a tree in the copse. Sometimes we even went to bed.

As time went on though we lost some of the passion and the romance and it seemed to me that it turned from, making love to having sex.

There is a difference Harry. In our latter years it became a regular Friday night thing. Every Friday night in fact. Every fucking Friday night Harry.

'That is what I called it the Friday Fuck.'

A quick ten minute fumble and bang and then you were asleep. Twenty-odd years of Friday nights, Harry. No matter how drunk you were, or how much you smelt of beer, stale beer. Friday night was fuck night. I had to drink a whole bottle of wine just to make myself endure it.

Where did the love making go, Harry? We had some romantic years before we got complacent. But we got on well. We worked, shopped, walked, ate, stayed in, went out together. You said that we had the same taste in clothing, furniture, films, food, books and even decorating the house.

Although I never told you did I, Harry? That the magnolia colour you painted every wall in the house? I always hated it. I wanted colour. But there it is now. Magnolia. Aah! well, what does it matter now? You are dead. I am alone. I am not sure I know how to be alone. I have never done it before. How am I going to cope without you?

Liz had left three over three hours ago and Paula had been sitting here alone for a long time just thinking, remembering.

Oh, yes the Hunt Ball was a night to remember. I was nineteen when we married you were twenty four. You had ambition, my Dad liked that at least. Mum liked you but they wanted us to wait a while before we got married. But we proved to them that we had endurance. Still a loving couple all these years later.

Sunday 4th April

When Paula woke to a bright sunny day it took a second for her to realise again that all was not right. She wondered if this was going to happen every morning and how long for. Waking up happy and then the cloud of despondency falling down on her. She had no idea what the time was but went for her morning shower and having dressed in a clean frock wandered down to the kitchen to put the kettle on the Aga.

'Oh Damn,' Better get some wood in as the Aga had gone cold. Heading to the back door and slipping her feet into her boots, she stopped and thought. I have a perfectly good electric hob, I can boil the kettle on that. Harry would not approve, but then Harry is not here to tell me off is he? She reasoned. Coffee, to start the day. She realised that she had not eaten more than a nibble of toast yesterday, but she still was not hungry. Just coffee it is them. She looked at the old kitchen and thought that it could do with a good paint up. How long since that dresser had been moved to clean behind it? The slate floor could do with a good scrub as well. Harry would not like to see it in such a state. He likes to see it all spick and span. Well he liked to see it that way, but Paula just couldn't bring herself to make the move to clean it. She just sat there with her coffee going cold.

'Are we going round to see your Mum today?' Eric asked Molly as they and their children were eating breakfast.

'Perhaps just Sandi and I should go? I don't want to overwhelm her.'

18

'I want to see Grandma, I want to give her a cuddle. Make her feel better.' Rachel said.

'Me to' piped in Daniel. 'It'll be strange without Grandpa there.'

In Sandi's house they were having a similar conversation. John thought it would be a good idea if they all went round at least for an hour or so.

'I'm just not sure how your Mum will be, but she shouldn't be alone all day.'

'What time are you planning to go round, that's if you are,' Sandi asked Molly on the phone.

'The kids want to come and see Mum.'

'Yes, so do mine but I am worried we may be a bit too much for her right now. Shall we go separately?'

'What do you mean too much? Anyone would think she was an invalid the way you talk about her. She isn't made of bone china, Molly. She is quite capable of telling us to go if she finds it all too much.'

'All right, don't jump on me. I have a huge bit of beef and we could all go round and cook her some lunch. I'm not sure she is eating anything.'

'Good plan, I'll do some veggies up and we can roast them as well. See you there about 11 o'clock?'

'Yep, sounds good.'

Paula was still sitting in the kitchen with her cold cup of coffee when they all arrived. They walked straight in as she had forgotten to lock the kitchen door.

'Mum, you really should be a bit more careful and remember to lock the door and the gate was open. Anything could have happened. Anyone could just walk in.' Molly told her.

It was on the tip of Paula's tongue to tell Molly to stop nagging at her, she had enough of that over the years from her father thank you very much. But she found she didn't have the energy.

Instead she accepted the offer of having Sunday lunch cooked for her and really quite enjoyed the rest of the day. There were a few tears from the children and the odd hushed mention of Dad but apart from that the afternoon had a good effect on the whole family. Just that empty chair!

Monday 5th April

Liz arrived at nine o'clock and she told me that the Detective Inspector wanted to come round. He had a few questions he needed me to answer. She called him to say it would be alright if he came now. I was up, dressed and had eaten breakfast, well half a piece of toast.. Probably, because I had not gone to bed. It didn't seem right without you there, Harry.

Liz said she was arranging for me to come to see you, maybe this afternoon.

'I have to warn you Paula, That Harry's wounds are extensive and he will not look, how shall I say it? At his best.'

I could feel the hysteria rising in me again. I had to see you, Harry. They have told me you were dead but I needed to see you, needed to be sure, I still couldn't believe it.

'Paula, had Harry consumed a lot of alcohol the night before he died?

I shrugged. 'Harry drank. He drank a lot.'

D.I. James arrived soon after and he sat down in Harry's recliner chair.

'Mrs Thompson. Firstly let me offer you my condolences at your great loss.'

Paula nodded in thanks.

'When we saw you the other day, you said you thought Harry had gone out about seven o'clock that morning. But the doctor though he had been dead for some twelve to fifteen hours.'

'I would often go to bed early and sometimes fell asleep before Harry came up. I assumed he had gone out rabbit shooting in the morning, he often did. They like to eat his cabbages and lettuces you see and he liked to shoot them. He would pop out before work sometimes. Annoying the neighbours. They are a long way off but sound carries. When I went up to bed, Harry was asleep in his recliner. That one.' Paula said indicating the chair that the D.I. was sitting in.

Oh yes, Harry, sleeping in your chair was quite normal. How often had I come down in the morning to find you still here and the T.V. still on. You worked so hard, too hard and got very tired. I would ask you to rest and say that you could have a heart attack or a stroke if you didn't slow down; and where would that leave me? Alone, Harry, just like now.

'Like I said when I woke in the morning I assumed Harry was already up and had gone to work. I didn't realise he had never actually come to bed. Which gun did he have?'

'A twenty bore lightweight shotgun.'

'My gun? Oh yes, he often took that one to shoot rabbits. Only in the grounds though. Wouldn't be seen out carrying a lady's gun.' Clay pigeon shooting you know. Harry was good at it. I wasn't so good but got along with it quite well.'

'The neighbour said he thought he heard shots late that night. You didn't hear anything?'

'Not a thing. I usually do but not that night, no. Where was he? Nobody has told me anything yet. All that I know is that my husband is dead.'

'Harry was found down by the copse. He was sitting by a tree. The gun, Mrs Thompson, was propped up beside him and he was found with his thumb on the trigger. We are working on the assumption that - erm - he sat down rather quickly and got caught up in the trigger mechanism. That's why we needed to know if he had been drinking. It will be ascertained at the post-mortem anyway but if, as you say, Harry drank a lot. Do you think he may have been drunk?'

'Harry rarely showed signs of being drunk, he just drank.'

'At this stage, working on the evidence so far, it would seem that this was a terrible tragic accident. Harry was not depressed was he?'

'No, he was never depressed, He was always the same, He loved life, his work, his family and me. He had been discussing early retirement. He was looking forward to being able to enjoy the fruits of our labour soon. No I don't think he was unhappy at all.'

Paula's head was starting to swim again and she could feel the bubbling in her stomach. She started shaking as she asked where the wound was on Harry.

'Mrs Thompson, the blast, it - erm - took the side of Harry's head off. He would have died instantly.'

'Oh goodness, Harry.'

Paula could feel the hysteria rising in her again and her shaking became uncontrolled. Liz looked concerned and asked if she could get anyone in to be with her.

'No, I will be okay. Don't disturb my children.'

'His face?' Paula asked.

'Is pretty much intact, um, one side anyway.'

'Who was the poor soul who found him? This is private land. A dog walker Liz said. It must have been a shock for them so perhaps they won't trespass on our land again. But that isn't important really is it?'

'Oh, poor Harry, it is so unfair, he worked hard all his life, we both had and now….now, oh good God what now?'

Paula's outburst silenced the inspector for a few seconds but he regained his composure and after a few more innocuous questions he left. And Liz said she would arrange for Pauline to see and identify Harry. Before she left she asked if Paula wanted transport for the visit.

'Do I need transport? Oh yes. I don't think I would've been able to drive to see you Harry. Feeling a bit shaky again I sat and stared out of the window until it got dark.'

23

D.I. James was not so sure about Paula's explanation of the events. Why had she not heard the shot? Did she take sleeping tablets? The copse was quite close to the house, close enough for a shot to be heard clearly. Her bedroom had a window facing the back of the garden toward the copse.

'I'm just not too sure about this one. It is of course entirely possible that he got caught up in the trigger when sitting down, but it would be very unusual for the gun to still be pointing at his head when it went off. And why didn't she hear anything?'

'Shall I check out if she was on any prescription drugs for sleeping? If I can that is. But of course there are also over the counter sleeping aids she could have taken,' Sergeant Willis answered.

'Yes, Willis, put someone on to it. I'm not saying I suspect her of killing him but it doesn't add up to me. Stranger things have happened. Check out her friends, neighbours, and family to see if we can find any motive for her or anyone to want him dead. When we get the post mortem back there might be some clues there. I'm always just a bit suspicious at such extreme reaction to such sad news. Of course she could have really loved her husband but in my experience it is usually because they are hiding something.'

Wednesday 7th April

It was as awful as they said it would be, seeing you Harry. Lying there, so pale with much of your face covered up. I didn't need to look under that cover, though they wouldn't have let me anyway. I was outside the room and someone in there just half pulled the cover back so that I could see the good bit of your face through a big window.

Molly and Sandi came with me, both crying, poor girls. I shook uncontrollably but did not cry. I have to remind myself that the girls are suffering as well and not let it all be about me. I formally identified the body lying there as you. My handsome man.

Paula left the mortuary where the body of her husband lay in a cold box. How long before she could bury him? She knew now that there was no hope of him ever returning, that he was gone forever. She had held out hope that it had all been a terrible mistake, that it had been someone else that had been found sitting up against a tree with half his head shot away. Molly and Sandi took her arm and escorted her to the waiting car that would take her home.

'We'll be over in a few minutes Mum, or would you prefer to come back to mine?' Molly asked.

Paula just shook her head and sat in the back seat of the police car. She couldn't understand why she had no feelings, why she wasn't crying or even raving at the unfairness of it all. But she had no feelings, either way. She thought that she must have something wrong with her as she had expected to be in tears at the very least, sobbing at her loss. She did feel sad that Harry had not lived for all his allotted years. But apart from that she felt nothing. Just heavy, as if she was carrying a huge weight around.

'Don't worry my darlings, I'll be fine. I just need to be home, where your Dad is.'

Sandi and Molly looked at each other at the car drove away. Sandi said. 'Well we all grieve in different ways. Mum just pretends to be strong, maybe for us. Coming? I'll drive us round to the house. John can get the girls from playschool.'

'Yeah, we can't leave her alone, not today, Molly answered with a sigh.

Monday 12th April

As Willis walked into D.I. Jones office he said.

'We have the P.M. report on Harry Thompson here sir. It would seem he was extremely drunk. Five times over the legal driving limit. It's a wonder he could walk straight with the gun in his hand let alone shoot anything. I expect if he was after rabbits he would have seen at least two of each one he tried to shoot.'

'Well our initial enquires show that they had a happy marriage and all the friends we have talked to have said that they were inseparable. Even to the point of living in each other's pockets, so to speak. I can't find any motivation to point to murder. He was well liked in the community and had a lot of friends who could vouch that they had an enviable relationship. I guess Mrs Thompson's melt down was genuine and she really is the grieving widow.'

'Nothing in his bank accounts that look suspicious?' Willis asked.

'No point trying to get a warrant to access his bank accounts if there is no motivation to kill him. It looks like a tragic accident. Not enough evidence to point to murder and no magistrate would grant a warrant on what evidence we have. I think I may have suspected the poor woman unfairly. I really think it was his drunken state that killed him. Mrs Thompson struck me as being rather needy? Is that a good way of putting it. Good job she has a supportive family, I would say. Feel quite sorry for her really. She doesn't look the type to be able to hold it together on her own.'

'So we close all further inquiries and send the report to the Coroner's court so it can be a full inquest?'

'Yes, let's get this wrapped up. Poor bugger shot himself. Good lesson there Willis. Don't go shooting rabbits when you have had a skin full.'

Friday 16th April

Today! The day for the Inquest. We will find out if the police are satisfied with their inquiry and if they think you took your life or had a terrible accident. I don't think they suspect murder at all since apart from annoying the neighbour every now and then with shooting rabbits, they have ascertained that you had no enemies. In fact everyone liked or loved you Harry. That is satisfying in itself.

Liz said that I will have to go to the witness stand but they will not ask me anything that has not already been asked. I feel the hysteria rising but must keep calm. I dress with care but do not put on any make up. I feel that I would probably cry it off. I have received many cards of sympathy, some phone calls and visits from friends. Yes Harry, you are well-liked - you were well-liked. I still use the present tense, maybe still in the hope that it is all a massive mistake.

When the inquest was opened, lots of people had to give evidence. Then it was my turn. Harry, you would have been proud of me.

I spoke clearly, answered all the questions and only broke down once.

I thought we would have to wait for a decision but the coroner made a speech. First she gave us her sincere condolences and then she said that from the evidence presented today she was satisfied that it was a tragic accident. That you had shot yourself, while trying to sit down by the tree, when your thumb got caught in the trigger mechanism of the gun.

Accidental death while under the influence of alcohol. Oh, Harry, how often were you told that that drink and tiredness would be the death of you, but not like this?

Sandi said. 'Liz, says Dad's body can now be released for the funeral. She asked which directors we want them to deliver him to. I said Morton's. Is that alright or do you want him to go somewhere else?'

'No Morton's will be fine and I will go in tomorrow to sort out his funeral.' You can both come if you like. But I don't mind if I go on my own.

'I'll come,' Molly said. 'Just to make sure you don't forget anything.'

So now there is something to focus on Harry, your funeral. I have to find out when it will be and let everyone know. Sort out somewhere to have your wake. I am not looking forward to it. But it will be a big do. You had so many friends and business acquaintances. Perhaps we will have the wake at home, people would like that. That's where I need to be and feel you there

Harry. You are still with me even though we are now talking about burying or burning you.

Monday 19th April

Oh, Harry. I have just had the most awful reminder that you are not here. The voting cards for the local council elections just landed on the door mat. Yours and mine. It is as if someone has poured icy cold water into my heart. To see your name on that card with your voting register number. I stood by the door looking at the card for what seemed like an age, crying, well sobbing really and shaking from head to toe. There is always post for you, most of it junk mail, but the other stuff goes straight to our solicitor, Mr Fraser, to deal with. But this, for some inexplicable reason has really shaken me up. Confirmation, Harry that you are not here to cast your vote.

Paula knew she had to phone the helpline number and let them know Harry had died.

I thought, do it now! But I was sobbing too hard and couldn't even hold onto the phone, let alone press the right buttons to get the number. It's a bad day, Harry. I miss you.

Of course you do, you can't manage without me and you know you can't.

Tuesday 20th April

Today I must get on the phone and find out what to do to have your name taken off the electoral roll. Yesterday was a bit of a shock, not only getting the voting card but my reaction to it. It was surprising at how much something like that would affect me. Yesterday has been cancelled as I didn't achieve anything, just sat indoors and cried on and off the whole day. Didn't eat and certainly didn't get dressed. Feeling so alone and it was also the first day that no-one came to visit me. Just me with my grief, my loss. It is probably just as well Harry, that no one came round because I don't think I would have been able to cope with them yesterday.

Feeling much stronger Paula decided to phone that helpline number to take Harry's name off the electoral role. Or at least find out what she had to do.

I spoke to a really nice lady who apologised for the fact that the card had been sent out. She said she couldn't find any entries to say that you had passed away. She said that they would need a death certificate. We had a long conversation and I found out that she had lost her husband very suddenly as well, so we had something in common. I said I thought our solicitor had all the death certificates and would get him to send one in. I got the address from her and she even gave me her name to mark the envelope to the attention of.

Although she was still close to tears Paula felt the need to get out of the house. But where? She could go for a walk, but she didn't want to go down to the copse.

Perhaps a walk into the village. It's only a couple of miles.

Will you come with me Harry? I feel you here in the house but not often when I am out, but we would do that walk together when you were still with me.

Paula thought that a walk to the village in the cool spring sunshine would be cheering. She phoned the girls who both said they would love to meet her in the pub for lunch.

Perhaps a walk in the fresh air will alleviate the puffiness around my eyes after all the crying I did yesterday. Harry, I wonder what you would have made of that. You didn't like to see me cry. You would cuddle me and comfort me when we were much younger. You always had a way to make me feel better and cheer me up. Crying was not allowed. Sadness was against the law. That's what you would tell me. I would ask what law? And you always said, 'Harry's law.'

That was when they were much younger, if Paula bursts into tears for any reason of late Harry would just sigh and walk off into another room. As if he couldn't bear to see her crying. So by Harry's law Paula set off for a walk to cheer herself up. It is still quite chilly but a lovely sunny day so she felt cheered by the brightness around her. The hedge rows she walked by had plenty of buds on that were opening with bright young leaves to welcome the summer and bring new life to the surrounding countryside.

She had gathered up her purse and phone, Well Harry's phone which Daniel had put her Sim card in. Harry had the latest smart phone, and Paula was learning how to use it. She had mastered taking pictures with it and saving them so on her way to the village she took some lovely photos of the burgeoning spring fauna. She thought she would be able to use them as studies to do some paintings with. She would down load them onto her computer when she got one but Daniel told her there was plenty of room on her phone, memory he called it, for as many pictures as she wanted to take.

Well when I get a computer that is, Harry. Oh the new technology, it is catching up with me. Or should that be that I am catching up with it? She thought as she walked along. She had been right, a simple walk in the countryside had cheered her up tremendously.

'Paula, my dear. However are you?' I heard about Harry, I'm so sorry you must be missing him so much,' said Mrs Patterson, who was the lady who kept the village shop.

Bugger, Paula thought, I was just beginning to cheer up and she has brought me right down again. But she is not going to spoil this day for me.

'Mrs Patterson, I am holding up as much as I can thank you.' Paula answered with a smile that really didn't fool anyone. The weight that was bringing her down was back. Bang went any happiness she may have been feeling.

'So what brings you out so far from home and on foot as well?'

'It's such a lovely day and let's face it there is nothing to keep me at home is there? Anyway I have been playing with Harry's phone and taking pictures on my way. Do you want to see?'

Paula clicked on to the phone's gallery and flicked through some of the pictures to show Mrs. Patterson.

'Don't you just love this time of the year?' she said in an attempt to lighten the mood again.

'Yes I always love the spring but autumn is my favourite time of the year. All the colours are so glorious. Don't you think?'

'Never been an autumn person myself.' Paula told her. 'After all what comes after autumn, just cold wet dismal winter. No, I much prefer spring with the promise of summer to come.'

'Yes I see your point. Well take care dear. If there is anything you need just let one of us know,' said Mrs Patterson, as she followed a customer into her shop.

Paula carried on towards the centre of the village and really enjoyed the rest of her walk to the pub.

'Well what do you think of that, husband barely cold and not even in his grave and she is out taking pictures of the sunshine.' Mrs Patterson said to the customer in her shop.

'No he hasn't been buried yet because there had to be an inquest.' Replied the customer.

'I heard they had to have an inquest because the police were not sure if he was murdered.' Mrs Patterson told her customer.

'I thought he was a likeable chap, can't see why anyone would want to murder him.'

'Perhaps it's closer to home. No smoke without fire is there? Why would there be a police investigation? You tell me that.'

' It was a sudden death though wasn't it?, They always have to investigate and have an inquest. Don't go reading too much into it Mrs Patterson, that poor woman has just lost her husband. What is she supposed to do stay indoors with the curtains shut? I think she is quite brave to venture out on her own, let's face it she has never been seen in here without her husband, never apart were they?'

Disappointed Mrs Patterson had to agree with her customer, there was no reason Paula shouldn't come out for a walk on a nice sunny day. So she had no scandal to gossip about in her shop and sorrowfully thought she would have to change her tack when discussing Paula with future customers.

Feeling much refreshed Paula arrived at the pub but could not see her daughter's cars there yet. What to do? Go in? On her own? That was something she had never done in her whole life. She had always had Harry with her when she went into a pub. There was always that thought that only certain women went into pubs alone. She knew she was being old fashioned and that in this day and age it was acceptable. She knew the pub and the people in there as she and Harry had walked down here often but she was very shy about going in alone. She walked further along into the village hoping in that time that the girls would arrive and she would be able to walk in and greet them. But on checking her watch she realised that there was another half an hour before she was due to meet them.

Well there was nothing for it she would have to go in, she could settle with a coffee and wait for them. So back she went determinedly, walked straight in the lounge and up to the bar.

'Morning there Mrs Thompson, how are you keeping? I'll just say it the once and that will be it. I'm very sorry to hear the sad news about Harry. Now what can I get you?'

'Oh that's very formal suddenly Bob. I'll have a cup of coffee for a start please,' she said.

'Right you are, Paula. Cup of coffee, coming right up.'

'The girls are meeting me so what delights do you have for our lunch then Bob?'

'Hang on a minute and I'll bring a menu over but I think Jo has some new specials up on the board as well.'

Well Paula felt a lot happier at her greeting in the pub and one of the old barriers to her becoming a lone woman had been removed. She didn't understand why she felt so loath to go into a pub, even the village local on her own but it was just one of those things women didn't do in her youth. Harry had always been very derogatory about women and girls who went into pubs alone. He associated them with, as he would put it, loose women. Paula realised that this was a very old fashioned even Victorian attitude and she had done it now and knew she could do it again. More and more doors were opening for her, more barriers being eroded. Life was opening up for her. Having met the girls for lunch in the pub including three glasses of wine Paula mused that it was a good job she had walked and not driven.

Harry would not have been pleased to come home to be told they had to fetch the car from the village.

'Sorry I couldn't make it to the funeral directors with you and Molly, Mum,' Sandi said. 'But I'm sure with Molly's help you will soon have it sorted.'

Paula thought that she really didn't need any help but kept that thought to herself.

'Mum, has decided to have the wake at home, she seems to think all Dad's friends would like that.' Molly didn't seem too pleased with the idea. 'I suggested having it here in the village pub so no mess to clear up, but she will have her way.'

'I am here you know, and it is my decision where the wake is. I'll get caterers in to do the food and drink. That way I won't have to worry about going home to an even emptier house.'

'Well, I think you're wrong but as you say it's your decision,' Molly said rather grumpily.

'Don't lets argue, I don't know about you two but I haven't cried yet today and I would like to get through one whole day without doing so if at all possible.'

'No, come on it's a lovely day and we are out to have lunch, that's a first for us. We haven't ever been in here just the three of us. Let's be ladies that lunch.' Sandi said.

'Okay, I'll drop the subject for now,' Molly conceded. 'What are you having I'm really hungry. What's on the specials board, Sandi, you can see it from where you're sitting.'

So lunch, decided and eaten with no further arguments all three women found they were actually enjoying each other's company. Soon it was time the girls went back to fetch their children from school.

Still the house felt so empty. Before Harry's death Paula was mostly there alone during the day but always looked forward to his arrival home in the evening. Now there would be no Harry walking in for his evening meal. Just as cold empty house.

It was as if Harry's death had taken the soul out of the house. It was just an empty shell of plaster and lath. It felt cold but not in a way that required Paula to put more cardigans on, it was an inner cold, one that crept into her bones into her heart and her own soul. She felt that the house no longer liked her and that she didn't belong there. She began to wonder if the house had ever really been hers. Legally it had always been just Harry's name on the deeds but it had been her home all these years. She had lived here longer than any other place. But was it her home? She just didn't know. Or was she just being fanciful?

Monday 3rd May
It's the day of your funeral Harry. You have been gone a month now and how I miss you.

Paula had been keeping herself busy with organising the funeral. She had decided that the house was a big enough venue to hold the wake and had found some caterers who would come in and set up food tables while they were all out at the crematorium.

She was expecting quite a lot of people to come to the funeral and the wake as Harry was a popular person in the town. They had their mutual friends and Harry had his own who would all be coming to say their goodbyes. Paula had looked though her wardrobe and found she had nothing suitable to wear or indeed nothing that fitted her.

She had lost a considerable amount of weight as apart from lunch out she was still not able to enjoy food. She decided she needed to go shopping for a funeral outfit.

She didn't want to wear black, Harry never liked her in black anyway, Navy was always his colour of choice for her. She found an acceptable suit in a blue colour which was much brighter than navy and with that she would wear a nice flowered blouse which had the same blue in it. It fitted her new shape perfectly and looked elegant.

Don't worry Harry, I am not about to flaunt my body in front of our friends. But I have come out of the flowing, billowing frocks, you liked me to wear. I feel they are no longer what I want. I have a shape and I wear clothes that fit it now. So when I get round to taking all your clothes to the charity shop those frocks will go too.

But of course having moved the frocks out there was a large space in her wardrobe to fill. She thought she may well drive to the city once the funeral was over and done with. She would buy herself some new clothes. She could go shopping in Harry's car. Of course she could also do online shopping as well.

Yes Harry I bought a laptop and have had a service provider connect me to broadband and Wi-Fi. I am coming into the 21st century. I need to know how to use it because although we have had computers at work you didn't like to bring work home. You stayed there to finish off the work often, except Friday nights. So you said there would be no need to have more than a basic computer at home and certainly no broadband.

She didn't know how to feel about this day, it would be their final long goodbye.

The end, the end of us. I miss seeing you sitting, well, slouching in your recliner chair, I still set the table for two sometimes but I refuse to clear it, I sit and eat my meal and pretend you are there telling me about your day. I would try to tell you about mine but I have never had anything interesting to say since stopping work. I'm not sure how much you listened to me anyway Harry. I have found some lovely photos of you, my handsome man, to put on your coffin at the service.

Of course there were her children to think about as well. Molly was coping quite well. Eric is very supportive and that helps. Sandi was going through an angry stage of her grief. But she could only rage at Harry and life in general and the whole unfairness of it all. Apparently grief has stages and that is just one of the stages Sandi will go through.

I so far have not passed the first stage. I feel the loss of you daily and find that in quiet moments I'm crying for no reason. I try to be alone when this happens to me not wanting to upset the girls more. But I also feel that Sandi thinks I don't care because apart from the first few days she has not seen my tears. I do cry but only when I'm alone. Sandi asked me why you had to be so bloody clumsy and shoot yourself. She thinks you drank because you didn't like being in our marriage, but we know that isn't the reason don't we Harry. You have always been a functioning alcoholic. This will be it, after today I will be expected to not show my grief any more.

Paula was beginning to feel stronger and that she wouldn't crumble into pieces. After today, all she had to do was carry on with her life. Without Harry.

 Oh Harry, you filled my life but now there is a great big hole where you were. Goodbye, my darling.

The service passed Paula by, she was in a dream like state and the only time she realised that she was paying any attention was when she glanced at the girls to make sure they were alright and not too upset.

When they got back there were quite a few people milling around the house and as it was a nice day in the garden. Some had wandered down to the copse to gruesomely look at the tree where their friend had met his death. Paula saw them and really didn't want them down there, it was her place, hers and Harry's. But she reasoned that they would want to go and see it even though it was somewhat macabre.

She made polite conversation with friends and business acquaintances of Harry's and even though she was not really there in her head she felt she had not done a bad job. She did keep taking surreptitious gulps of her wine to fortify herself and was surprised that she was not drunk, with the amount she had consumed. At last it was over and they had all left apart from the family. Sandi had left the twins with John's parents who looked upon it as the perfect excuse not to come to the funeral. Not that they didn't want to say goodbye to Harry but they said that funerals were becoming a constant in their lives and one more they could do without. Eric went and picked Daniel and Rachel up from school. Molly didn't want them to be at the service but thought they would be able to cope with the wake.

Paula was surprised at the roller coaster of the day. It had started with sadness and then blinding misery at the service, with her just about holding herself together. To a party like atmosphere, when they all got back to the house. There were many stories and anecdotes of Harry from friends old and newer which made every one laugh. He had been well liked and was always the life and soul of any gathering. Paula found herself actually laughing quite a lot at some of the antics that were attributed to her husband.

It seemed to Paula that Harry had lots of friends, some of which she had never known. But they obviously knew him very well. It made her feel a bit isolated as there were jokes and stories being bantered about that she had no part in.

She decided to wander in the garden alone and wished they would all go away. How could she feel like an outsider at her own husband's funeral?

How did it get to the point where I knew so little about you Harry? And how did it get so far that you really didn't know me?

Paula thought she should go back in but not to socialise, to get another drink.

Tuesday 6th May

Well, it was over, Harry had been burned up, and his life had been drunk to. There was quite a party after the service and lots of people had stories to tell about him.

I wonder who that woman was at the service? I didn't recognise her. She didn't come back to the house. Sandi didn't know her but Molly said she had seen her somewhere.

'I know who that woman was, you know the one at the funeral service? Her boy is in Rachel's school. He is a year older I think but I've see her there.' Molly told Eric.
'So what was she doing at the service? Eric asked. 'Can't see how your Dad would have known her.'
'Well, he obviously did know her or she has some kind of funeral fetish. She looked quite young, not of Dad's generation, so unlikely to be a friend as such.'
'My thoughts exactly,' Eric said.

Paula was wondering if the furnace burned extra hot with all the alcohol in Harry's body or had it dissipated by that time?

That is the sort of joke you would have told. Silly, but quite funny, in its way. Isn't it odd how the mind works? I would never have thought of something like that, it must be you coming out in me.

Paula had told herself that she must get on with life now the funeral was over and decided she would take a trip into town. She wanted to pick up some colour charts.

Any colour, as long as it wasn't magnolia. Also, she needed some new clothes. Some nice tops and jeans. After all she was only in her fifties, not a pensioner yet and didn't need to dress like an old person any more. Before she even set out she could feel Harry's disapproval. It would be strange going shopping without Harry there to guide her and give his opinion on what suited her.

She took Harry's car just to feel that bit closer to him. Some time back when Harry had the electric gates fitted there were two fobs to go on the key rings and Harry still had the old fob on his. Paula had never had a fob on her car key ring as Harry had said that the extra one should stay in the house in case. In case of what Paula never did establish.

But she would have to drive close to the button to open the gate to go out and when she came home she would have to get out of her car to open the gate as the button was not close enough for her to reach from her car window. One time the gate had broken down and she had stood in the pouring rain trying to open it. This experience had brought on a nasty cold which had quickly turned in to a very nasty illness similar to pneumonia. She had been in bed for some weeks and Harry had to do all the housework and look after her. It was soon after that incident that Harry had changed the gates to have them fully automatic but able to lock them from indoors for security. Both Molly and Sandi had remotes to unlock the gates as well just in case.

I was actually up really late last night when everyone had gone home, Harry. I missed your snoring but I was

43

playing with my laptop. I have joined a few social media sites and have already found two old school and college friends. Some of us are going to meet up in a few weeks. That will be fun. Oh, and later on this week I will go and cast my vote. I have decided who I am going to vote for. As it happens, I think you would have voted for him as well. But this is my decision, based on my own research. I looked at all the leaflets that came through the door and went online to see if I could find anything out about the candidates and then I make my mind up which I was going to vote for. I am getting quite independent.

There was still a hole in Paula's life. She came home to an empty house and she knew that would never change. He was never going to be there, to greet her or come in to be greeted by her. She missed having him around, even if he didn't talk much but was just sitting there drinking. She realised that when Harry did talk it was usually to give her instructions or tell her that she had done something wrong. Or at least, something that was not to his liking.

First thing in the morning when I turn for a cuddle and your side of the bed is cold. Preparing meals, although I eat differently now, much more healthily, I think and I am still losing weight. I feel so much better without all that flab. You used to like to get hold of it and give it a squeeze but you would be hard pushed to do it now. I don't have the daily paper now either.

I used to like to do the crossword with you, it's no fun alone. Is life much fun on my own? I don't know. I have to make decisions for myself. I am not sure I am ready for that. I still have a cry most days, it will just suddenly catch me and then I am blubbing and a great sadness overcomes me, then I have to go upstairs and re-apply my make-up. Yes, Harry, make up. I wear it every day now, not to make me feel better, but just because I want to. You didn't like me to wear it much, I know, but I like how it makes me look, and feel.

They had spent so many years together and her life had merged into his. Now he wasn't there it was, she thought, as if half of her had been torn away. She felt half a person and no longer complete.

Sunday 23rd May

It's your birthday and I have made you a cake. We are having a tea party today for the grand-children. They have all made birthday cards for you and we have put them up on the dresser just as if you would be in any time to see them. Everyone is here. I have made sandwiches, scones, cupcakes and lots of tea. I have pulled the big quilted bed cover down and laid it on the floor so we can have a picnic, indoors. It's a pity it is raining or we could probably have gone on the lawn for our tea. It's been wet for a few days now and the ground is soggy. So am I sometimes because I have been caught out in the rain a few times lately.

We would often have indoor picnics when the girls were little. You would be down there on the floor with us, chucking buns at them and making a right royal mess. Last year though when we did it you sat in your recliner and watched, saying, 'I'm too old to be crawling around the floor.'

You were also late home from work that day and nearly missed all the fun. I remember that you didn't really engage with the children at all. I wondered why you were so late home. Had you been somewhere else? I asked but you told me not to interfere and to leave you alone. I know Molly thought that was a bit odd, and flashed a look at Eric. Did they know something? Now I wonder if it had something to do with that woman at your funeral. I had a funny feeling about her.

Well today we are going to have our indoor picnic and I have put a plate of food on your recliner chair, so you can be with us. There is also a large glass of your single malt.

Molly, Sandi and I are having a glass or two of wine. A toast to you, my, darling and the life we had together. I miss you.

When the children finished their tea the rain had stopped so they went to play out in the garden where Eric and John tried to supervise a game of cricket. Paula, Molly and Sandi walked down to the copse and stood for a while by the tree that Harry had been sitting against on the fateful morning. Paula thought she could still feel his presence there but there were times in the house when he was fading away from her. Sandi was crying gently and she said that she was surprised at how much she was missing Harry.

'I've been married for more than five years, have children of my own but I really miss having him about. Just the chat to and cuddle.'

'Of course you do, no one expects to lose their Dad quite so young.'

Molly said. 'I miss him too, his silly jokes, when he use to dress up as Father Christmas and pretend to be offended when we pulled his false beard off.'

'Yes, and the chocolate cakes at tea time, when he would cut all the chocolate off and hand us the cake and say that he had taken the tax off already.' Sandi added.

'Or what about when he decided he no longer wanted the chickens and had them all butchered, even the one Molly had made into a pet. I can remember next time we had roast chicken you looked at him and said "Brownie is looking at you" and he couldn't eat it.'

'Oh, Mum, did I? How awful, poor Dad.'

'I'm sure he forgave you. I don't like looking at that tree. I want to have it felled but I am afraid I will lose him forever if I do and that is the last tie to him.'

'He's gone Mum. The tree didn't kill him anyway, it just bears the scars.'

'Yes, and here we say goodbye.'

The cricket game was going well but some more fielders were needed so the mother and daughters headed back to the lawn to play with the children.

'I have booked a riding lesson.' She said rather too brightly to the girls as they walked back up the garden to join in the cricket game.

'Good for you, Mum,' Sandi said.

'Sure you are not too old to be doing that now?' Molly asked.

Paula was saved from needing to answer that by a shout from the top of the garden.

'Grandma catch,' Daniel yelled, as the ball came flying towards them. By sheer fluke Paula caught it and John's innings came to an end. As it had started raining again they headed indoors and cleared up the picnic tea. Zoe and Dee were getting tired and Sandi said. 'That was lovely, happy birthday Dad. And what do we say to Grandma for the lovely cakes and buns she cooked for us all?'

'Thank you Grandma,' Chorused the two little girls. And Rachel piped in as well. Daniel said 'Yeah thanks Grandma.'

Paula thought to herself. 'Oh gosh he is growing up. Will he be like you Harry? He certainly has your looks.'

When Paula was alone again she marvelled at the fact that she didn't need to cry. The house was empty apart from her and the ghost of Harry. There was no feeling of him there today even with it being his birthday. She wondered how long it took a presence to fade away, or was it up to the individual? Tonight she was at peace and sat down to watch a bit of Sunday night television.

She got her lap top and started looking for clothes for the over fifties. After all she can't just wear jeans or her one good suit for ever. She wanted stylish, tasteful clothes. Nothing too young but nothing frumpy either, and bright colours.

Oh no, Harry this lady is going shopping. What is it they say? Shop till you drop? Well that will be me. Better still I will go to that big outlet and spend a day or two there. Just shopping. They have a hotel I could stay in.

Tuesday 25th May

Having phoned both her daughters and told them of her plans for the next couple of days Paula packed two big empty suitcases into the back of Harry's car and a small overnight bag. She then set off for the big new out of town outlet she had read about. It was only about an hour's drive away but if she was going to be shopping she thought she may as well stay over for at least one night. A chance to get away. Another first. She had never stayed in a hotel without Harry before. This would be an adventure. She had to be home for Friday as that was when she had booked her riding lesson.

All these shops, Paula was enthralled. She spent the first morning just browsing. Then in the afternoon after a light lunch she started shopping as if her life depended on it. She started at one end of the top floor and bought something she liked in each shop. She also made sure she picked up a catalogue or brochure in each shop in case she fancied something else when she got home and could order it on line. She was having so much fun.

She made her way back to the hotel and spent a happy hour or so trying on all these clothes again together and then would have an idea of what else she might need for the lower floor tomorrow.

Time for some dinner. So having made sure she had removed all the labels she put on a nice new, not too dressy outfit and went down to the hotel restaurant to have some dinner. This was nerve racking, something else she had never done. She popped a book in her bag so that she would have something to do rather than sit there alone like a lonely no mates.

'May I sit here?' A strong male voice asked.

Paula was surprised when looking up from her book she saw a very handsome man hovering by her table.

'Yes, if you like,' she said looking around to see that there were in fact plenty of seats spare. So why would he want to share her table?

As if he read her mind he said. 'I expect you are wondering why I asked to share with you. You look as if you are travelling alone as I am and I hate dining alone.'

'Well if I am to have company I will put my book away. My name is Paula.'

'Nice to meet you Paula. I'm James.'
He was a business man who didn't like to but needed to travel sometimes. He said he often stayed in this hotel as some of the clients he had to visit were in this area.

'Can I get you a drink?'

'Thank you no, I have some wine here and I am just having the one tonight. I've so much on tomorrow. I have some serious shopping to do.'

'Where is your husband? I wouldn't expect a lovely lady like you to be here alone?'
Paula thought quietly to herself that he was a bit patronising but she realised that most men of his age were like that. In fact Harry would often comment on women out alone in much the same manner.

'He died. So I am alone. Just getting away from all the rush and having some me time.'

The conversation went on through the meal and James offered Paula a coffee, but as she headed towards the bar he took hold of her arm and tried to direct her to the lift saying, 'I have coffee in my room. I'm sure I can offer you more than that as well.'

'I'm sorry James you seem to have wasted your time here. I came here to be alone and do some shopping, nothing else. I will not be going to your room for coffee but will be pleased to accompany you to the bar to have one if you wish to continue to drink.'
She thought she had by-passed a rather awkward situation and was pleased that she made her point.'

'Oh don't flatter yourself, lady I felt sorry for you, sitting there pretending to read your book, don't say you weren't on the lookout for a quickie. I don't normally go for the older woman but I thought you needed a bit of attention. Go to your lonely room and have your, me time, but don't go leaving it too late my dear, you won't be getting too many more offers as good as this one.'

With that he stalked off to the bar leaving Paula in shock. She stood right outside the lift wondering what the hell had just happened there. He was quite good company over dinner but she felt very insulted that he would expect her to jump into bed with him, and further add insult he had come out with that tirade when he realised she was not what he thought.

Paula caught the lift and went to her room. She was upset by the encounter but more confused. She certainly had a lot to learn about the world today. Harry had always told her that no one would want her apart from him. Was he right? It would seem if she just wanted sex she could get that whenever she wanted, but was that want she wanted? Did she want another relationship? It was far too early to think like that anyway. But in the future would she want to share her life with someone again? She thought the answer to that one would be a resounding no. She was just finding her feet, even though she was still missing Harry and grieving for him, she had been enjoying her independence. But she now knew she had so much to learn having been sheltered by Harry for so long. She resolved to go home in the morning and give herself more time to get used to living the life of an independent woman. The whole episode has unnerved her so much. In fact it has scared her.

Tuesday June 1st
Today at quarter past five in the morning I came down for a cup of tea, I've been awake for a while. Yesterday I started sorting out your clothes and found a few packets of cigarettes in your pockets. I just lit one and smoked it. I feel a bit dizzy now and dry in my throat. I don't like it so I won't do that again. I'll have to throw them away. There was another mobile phone. I'm not sure why you would want two of those, but there is a lot about you I'm beginning to realise I didn't know.

I also found some condoms. They were in date so I can't understand why you would want them either. I am well past the time when protection is necessary, so they were obviously not meant to be used with me. Who then Harry? That woman? At the funeral? I have seen her again, in town. She looked as if she wanted to speak, but I didn't stop. I don't want to know if she had anything to do with you. Molly has seen her as well, standing looking at the warehouse. Just standing there!

It was the day set aside for a big clear out of Harry's clothes. Paula had also collected a few of Harry's more cherished items for Molly and Sandi to look through to see if there was anything they wanted. His wardrobe was cleared as well as his bed room drawers and all those clothes were bagged up ready for the charity shop run. She had set aside some rather nice shirts to ask the girls if Eric or John would like them. But although very fine quality and expensive they were not very fashionable, so she didn't expect any one to take them.

Paula had reluctantly come to the sad conclusion the Harry was never coming back to her.

So, today we are clearing you out of the house Harry and tomorrow I have a second riding lesson. I don't think I am too old despite what Molly said.

You know I used to ride, in fact when we met I had a couple of horses and you said that you tried to love them as I did Harry but horses were not your thing. You were nervous around them. You also asked why I would want them as I had you now and they would be a distraction from our work. You said that if we work hard now and make enough money then we could have whatever we want later. I would have a horse again at some point. It made sense, so we gave up everything and worked and worked.

At some point I thought when were wealthy enough to step back a bit I would go back to riding. But you felt the need to make the business even bigger.

Eventually, when we did start having some spare time you took up clay pigeon shooting again and I came along with you. You said I would enjoy it and you were right, I did. We got good at it and entered competitions. I didn't win many but you did. You also bought a yacht and we went sailing. That was fine on the river but I didn't like it when we went to sea. I was sick.

But we never got round to getting me another horse. When would we have time for it? You asked. But I asked, 'When would be my time? Well, Harry, I would have had time but you wanted me to be with you. But now, now is my time and I am going riding. On a horse I have never ridden before.

I loved my riding and was quite competitive. I went hunting and did cross country jumping. You came with me once to a show but I could see you were bored and then refused to come again. I felt guilty at leaving you to do your own thing on Saturday or Sunday to be with my horses. You complained that they took up a lot of my time. Our time, you said. I let my friend have my pony and when my old horse died I just sort of hung up my boots.

Every now and then a friend would offer me a ride but you always had other plans for us so I didn't go very often. I wanted another one but there never seemed time. I was about ready to buy one when I fell pregnant with Molly, then Sandi came along so I haven't ridden for nearly thirty years. I am going for a half hour lesson, just to see how I get on. I found my boots in the attic but have no jodhpurs, so will have to ride in stretch jeans. I am sure the riding school will have a hard hat that will fit me.

I thought I would go on a week day so at least there won't be loads of kids around to watch this old woman who thinks she can still ride. Not quite so embarrassing that way. Would you come and watch me Harry? I suspect you wouldn't. In fact I really think you would find something else for us to do instead. I just want to ride a horse again, to wander around the country side on horseback. I don't want to compete again just a quiet hack out.

I was a good rider, back in the day. I won cups and rosettes. They are still in the attic. I refused to chuck them away every time you decided to have a clear out. Even though they were, as you pointed out, from a past life. As soon as we could afford it you started buying more guns and we were going shooting when we couldn't sail. But I never had another horse. You promised when we could afford it I could get one but a clothes horse was the closest I got to having one.

But now Harry is my time and I am going riding.

Sunday 6th June

'Oh my goodness, I still ache.'

'Oh dear Mum, I suppose it will take a few times to retrain your riding muscles.' Sandi answered. She had phoned to see how the riding lesson had gone.

'But did you remember how to do it? Is it like riding a bike, once learned, never forgotten?'

'Well I didn't do too badly, even if I do say so myself. I do find going upstairs a bit of a challenge with my sore legs but I am going again today and that will sort out those muscles.'

'Oh brilliant, another lesson?'

'Yes, one more then I'll go out for a proper ride.'

'Well have fun, coming round for tea tomorrow? We can't get over this afternoon and anyway you are forsaking us for horses.'

'God, you sound just like your father there.'

'Really? Gosh. Better watch my step. See you tomorrow after school or do you want to pick the girls up?'

'Yes, I'll do that, and bring them home to you.'

Sitting here Harry thinking of how much I am going to enjoy my next lesson brings back such memories. When I was the girl you first met and fell in love with. The go getting, full of energy, bright, cheerful and I must say popular girl who was swept off her feet by you. I could say my, 'Knight in shining armour', but firstly you didn't like horses so you couldn't ride along on your white charger, and secondly you didn't rescue me did you Harry? You lured me into a trap.

Monday 7th June

I'm not nearly so achy today. I really enjoyed my lesson. Oh horses I am back!

How did you keep me away from this for so long Harry? I didn't realise how much I missed it until I got back in that saddle. Today is a good day, I can almost say I am happy, really happy. It's such a long time since I felt really happy Harry. I don't think you ever made me feel like this. I am beginning to get so much more energy back as well. I am sitting in the car outside Zoe and Dee's school, waiting until it is time to go in and get them. I love picking them up and being with all the young mums. I'll stop by the bakers and get some cakes on the way to Sandi's house. Besides there is rather a nice dress shop next to the bakers in town, and I may just have a look in there to see if there is anything I simply must have.

'Hi, Sandi. Mum here. I'll just pop to the bakers on the way back to yours and have a quick look in the dress shop. So we may be a bit late. Just so you don't worry. See you soon.'

Paula left this message on both Sandi's home phone and her mobile. At least she was covered for a while to go shopping with the girls. Zoe and Dee picked the cakes for themselves and decided which ones Mum, Dad and Grandma should have then spent a happy half hour picking out nice things for Grandma to wear in the dress shop. Luckily Paula was in agreement with most of the little girls choices and bought a blouse Dee really liked and a jumper that took Zoe's fancy. Along with a new pair of jeans and some other tops. Laden with shopping they went back to the car and loaded them in the boot.

Shutting the boot of the car Paula glanced up to see a woman looking right at her, that same woman who had been at Harry's funeral. She had a little boy with her, about Rachel's age. Paula hurried to strap the two children into their car seats and drove off back to Sandi's house. She could not understand why that woman would be staring at her. Why did it bother her so much? Who was this woman and why was she at Harry's funeral service? She had not come back to the wake, so can't have known him that well, but why go to the service? It was a puzzle and no mistake.

'Did you notice that woman at Dad's funeral?' Paula asked Sandi as soon as the girls had gone to play. 'I saw her again today and she had a little boy with her. She stared at me. I get the feeling I should know her? But I can't place her at all.'

'Molly mentioned something about her but I don't know her at all, as far as I know.'

'She makes me nervous, I can't think why but I keep seeing her.'

'Molly did mention that her son goes to Rachel's school. Perhaps you have seen her there when you have been picking up Rachel?'

'No, it's more than that, she has something to say I'm sure but I don't think it's something I want to hear. If you see what I mean.'

'Now, Molly will say you are becoming paranoid. I'm sure there is nothing in it.'

Paula was not reassured by this conversation and as soon as tea had been eaten she made her excuses and went home.

'Mum seems very edgy about that woman at the funeral. Says she keeps seeing her and feels that the woman has something to say to her,' Sandi told John.

'Is that why she went home so early? She usually likes to put the girls to bed when she's here. I don't know who this woman is but didn't you say Molly had seen her?'

'Yeah, I will have to ask Molly about her, Mum is getting quite paranoid. Are the girls asleep?'

Wednesday 16ᵗʰ June

Harry, it is our anniversary. We would have been married 33 years today. I have never been so long alone without you. No-one has remembered except me. It's not something the girls thought about. Not since they had their own weddings and children. That's understandable.

But I remember and I am sitting here with all sorts of feelings bombarding me.

Sadness that you are not here to celebrate with me. Sadness that I am alone and have no plans to go out. No celebratory dinner with red roses and champagne. Getting dressed up to go out to a smart restaurant, coming home to make love both of us rather drunk.

That's exactly what I am going to do now. I'm going to get drunk on my own and pretend you are here with me. I can stay in bed all day tomorrow there is no need for me to be anywhere. So I start on the wine that was in the pantry. I have had several glasses and my head is rather dizzy. I know I am drunk and don't care. I can see you Harry. I can feel you touching me. I begin to become aroused at the thought of your touch. How it used to be when we were young, first married and so much in love with each other's bodies. You would just give me a look and I would begin to feel excited. Now, Harry I can imagine your touch, wanting your touch. Are you with me? I feel closer to you than I have for years. Even though you are not here in person. Will I ever enjoy sex again? Does it matter? All these questions and you can't answer them for me can you? I do feel hot and horny but I am drunk. Very drunk Harry. The kind of drunk you didn't like to see and sitting here talking to you as if you are really here and I can see the look of disgust on your face at the state of me. Funny that, as you would drink all the time and although you never got staggering drunk, you were never really sober where you? But I can also feel you looking at me with that look the one that would get me going. Get me tightening and wanting you. Ohhh Harry.

Paula, Paula, Paula, just look at you. You are a mess. You know I always hated to see you drunk, it's not becoming on a woman of your age. Whatever have you done to yourself, you are far too thin already and I expect you think you look attractive like that. Well go ahead my lovely and try to be attractive but no one else will want you. And as for making love to you. Not in that state my dear.

Thursday 17ᵗʰ June

I don't want to get up today Harry. I feel terrible needing water and feeling sick. It wasn't just the one bottle of wine, I drank nearly two. All by myself. I am really badly hung-over. Just have to cancel today and try to sleep it off. Tomorrow it will have passed.

Oh I did let myself go last night and did something I have never done before. Is that what they call spiritual sex? Or was it just drunken wantonness? Oh well back to sleep if I can and get over it.

Will you come and cuddle me, Harry?

You disgust me.

Friday 18ᵗʰ June

Paula woke early to find that the hangover headache had gone. She realised that she was hungry but of course having spent the day in bed yesterday she had not eaten anything all day. Shower and breakfast, she thought. It was such a lovely day that she ate her toast and had her coffee outside in the sunshine. She had to get busy as she was meeting one of her old school friends in town today. One that she had found on social media. They had not seen each other for many years and joked that each would wear a flower in their lapel and carry a copy of the Sun. On her way indoors to get ready she picked a flower.

I'll have to pick up a copy of the paper from the shop on my way, she told herself.

She wore a short sleeved summer frock that fitted her figure with matching shoes that have a small heel, she didn't want to go tripping over in stilettos. She was looking forward to seeing her old friend but still had reservations and was nervous. Something else she had not done on her own for many years.

They were meeting in a pub in town which was known for its lunch time trade. Well, that's no problem now, Paula thought. I have broken the ice of walking in a pub on my own.

It turned out to be unnecessary because as she pulled in to the pub car park she saw a woman about her age getting out of a car on the other side. She recognized Julia immediately and walked over, brandishing her copy of the sun.

'Paula, Oh God you have not changed one little bit.'

'Well I knew it was you straight away, how fantastic is this?'

So with arms linked the two ladies went into the pub for a light lunch and some heavy conversation full of memories, reminiscences, and jokes.

'I still haven't said I'm sorry about Harry, have I?' Julia said when the conversation calmed down a bit.

'What a shock it must have been for you.'

Paula felt tears close by but held them back with a great effort.

'I lost more than just my husband, I lost my soul mate, and he was like another half of me,' she answered. 'But I have to carry on now and find out how to live without him.'

Julia patted Paula's hand and told her again how sorry she was. 'I think I know how you feel, I'm not sure how I would cope with out Jim. He is my rock. But you are starting off very well, It was so nice to be able to get in touch now that you have an media outlet as the kids say.'

'Is that what they call it? We just had phones at home didn't we?'

'And school discos.'

With the mood lightened again Paula felt the weight of grief lighten again.

'How many of the convent girls have you kept in touch with? she asked Julia.

'Well, there is Ann, Theresa and Philly. We should all meet up and see if we can get any more. I'm sure they must have contact with some of the others and we could have a convent old girls lunch. I know some of the others have to work during the week. But we must be able to find a day when we can all get together.'

The lunch ended with promises of meeting up again and arranging time for a big girly lunch.

Whatever did I worry about? Thought Paula, on her way home. She had a lovely time and really enjoyed meeting up with her old friend again. With the promise of finding some more of her buddies she really felt again that doors were opening for her. She began to realise how oppressive her marriage had been, how Harry had kept such a tight rein on her that he had reduced her world to fit only him in it.

 Oh don't get me wrong, Harry. I would never have changed you but you changed me and I am finding just how free life can be without you.

We will see Paula, we will see.

Thursday 1st July

It's already July and we would be thinking about upcoming holidays. Devon? Cumberland? Liverpool? It has occurred to me that we never went on a holiday abroad together. You always said there was so much of our own country to see, I would often bring brochures home of foreign holiday places or cruises. But you studiously ignored them. You never wanted to get on a plane, or a ship. It was as much as I could do to get you on a train.

   You would pack up the car and we would drive. We stayed in some wonderful hotels and were treated like royalty as you would when paying for five star accommodations. I used to love going abroad when I was with my parents, they always made sure we had a foreign holiday at least once a year. You just would not go. My parents even paid for us to go with them to a lovely villa in Spain one year but you said you had work commitments. I said I would take the girls but, oh, Harry, how you sulked. How would you cope without me for two weeks? How could I take our daughters away from you for so long? You would miss us terribly. So in the end we didn't go. We all stayed home and you went to work.

We did have some lovely holidays when the girls were little though. We had some really fun times. I did manage to get you across the water one time when we went to Cork. We took your car and went on a ferry from south Wales. I remember it was not a drive on ferry they lifted the car up and put it in the hold with a big crane.

We stood on the quay watching and you held your breath until the Jaguar was safely down in the hold.

It was an overnight trip so once we had got the girls settled in their cabin we went for a drink and then made love to the swaying of the boat.

I remember that there were road works all over the place but never any one working them. But overnight they would miraculously get done and cleared away. We thought it must be leprechauns who were doing the work.

The weather was with us on that holiday but the beaches were full of jelly fish so the children couldn't go swimming. It was a good holiday though; we had lots of good ones all over the British Isles. Never abroad!

The girls go somewhere abroad, with their children every year. Well if they want a babysitter with them I will go as well, but would have to get a passport sorted out.

Then we had our caravan. You loved that. Self-catering, you said was the way to go. Yes I can remember cooking a complete Sunday roast in that caravan, while you took the girls fishing. Neither of them will have a caravan now, so I am not sure how much they enjoyed it. Obviously not as much as you did, Harry, and to be honest it meant quite a lot of work for me. I still had to provide three meals a day, and clean. I had to stock the caravan, sort out all our clothes for the week and wash them all and the sheets and bedding when we came home. In fact the caravan was not a holiday for me.

Well I am not going anywhere this year at least I have no plans to at the moment. Having found my riding again there no desire to go abroad and miss my lessons. Well maybe not, I may change my mind.

I will have the grand-children when the girls go away and we will have fun in the garden, and out to zoos and other local attractions. We are going to camp out in the garden so I have been and bought a huge tent, camping stove, air mattresses and everything we need for staying in the great outdoors. All four of them, at the same time. We never did that. We could have two one week then two the next but never all together. Harry, you might have been useful here for that holiday week, to have you here to help entertain the kids.

No, Paula, looking after children was your thing, I would have stayed at work and everything would be cleared away by the time I came home. You know I hated all those toys lying about. It always had been your job to look after the children and the house and my job was to make sure you do it properly.

Sunday July 4
As the weather was so nice Paula decided to have a trial run of camping in the garden with the children. She had been out to a camping shop and bought a big family tent which had a kitchen area and two curtained off bedrooms. She bought airbeds and sleeping bags. Three pretty pink ones for the girls and a masculine dark blue

one for Daniel. Paula decided she would use one of the new duvets from indoors that she had already bought as she just didn't fancy being trussed up in a sleeping bag. Cooking items, a fridge that would stand in the tent and a stand to put a washing up bowl in. She and the salesman from the camping shop had great fun trying to fit all this in the car. She had to call Eric and John to help her put up the tent it was too big for one person to do alone.

She then had to work out how to get lights and power for the fridge and some way to have music. That was easily sorted with a long extension from indoors. She put a bucket over the sockets just in case it rained. When all that was ready she went shopping for food that she knew the children would love to eat while camping. Then she was all set.

The children arrived straight from school Friday evening, brought by their Mums. Molly inspected everything to make sure it was as safe as it could be. She was not entirely happy with the extension covered with a bucket but as no rain was forecast she let that one go. Eric had found an old tarpaulin which he brought and laid down the slope of the lawn. He then fixed the garden hose so that water could trickle down the home made water slide for the children to play on.

Paula really enjoyed her weekend alone with the children, she took hundreds of pictures with her new tablet and Daniel showed her how to send them to Molly and Sandi. She was getting the hang of this new technology and loving it.

Computer, tablet, laptop and smart phone I have them all now. You always said that you had enough of them at work, that home should be a computer free area. But I can keep in touch with people from all over the world with the computer Harry. I get a lot of pleasure from it. So all in all it had been a good weekend and the children had gone home now for long hot bath and bed.

Daniel had mentioned that he was too big to be sleeping with the girls and he would rather have a tent of his own. Paula decided she would go back to the shop and get him a single man tent just for his bedroom in the garden. If he wants to be the man of the house then let him. Paula could perfectly understand how he would want some time alone being the only boy and he did consider himself so much more grown up than his sister and of course his younger cousins.

Tuesday 6 July
Probably time to order oil for the heating tank. I usually do at this time of the year, and this year I will fill it up, so I know I have plenty when I need a bit of heat in the house.

I had better get the boiler serviced as well. I need to check your address book to find the number of the nice chap who came to do it last year. One of the many jobs you took from my shoulders, Harry. Things you said I need not worry about. I have been checking through your address book and have noticed some entries in there that mean absolutely nothing to me.

They don't look like business numbers as they just have an initial beside them and not a company name. Oh well, I am sure if I need them for anything I will find out who they are. I can't say I really want to know.

I have created a file on the computer for important numbers so then I can burn your address book. Oh, and I saw that woman again. She really looked as if she wanted to speak. Nice looking woman and the child is a good looking boy Whoever is she? I have never seen her before the funeral but now she seems to be everywhere.

Wednesday 28th July

I have been checking that the air beds are blown up in the tent and putting new bedding on them. I have also checked that Daniel's tent is still up, it was a bit windy last night. I will be sleeping in the big one tonight with Zoe, Dee and Rachel. As they are coming over this afternoon for the start of our garden camp out week.

You should see the garden Harry. It is a really fun place to be. I have bought giant dominoes, chess, noughts and crosses and a huge monopoly game. All these are laid out on the lawn for the children to play with. Or not, if they don't want to. I really don't care. We will have picnics, storytelling and dance competitions. I have set up a target as well for the bows and arrows

Daniel and Rachel are coming tomorrow, so tonight it is just me and the little ones. I hope they don't miss their mum too much, but I will keep them entertained until they fall asleep.

Fun times! Harry fun with my grandchildren. The school holidays are going to be so much fun. I know the children are looking forward to it anyway. I may feel a bit uncomfortable as I am used to my big fluffy bed.

Thursday 29th July

The girls were so excited last night Harry. We had burgers and then we had some storytelling and they went to bed in the big tent. I stayed up reading by the light of the big lamp which also plugged into the extension lead under the bucket.

Fry up for breakfast and then we await the arrival of the bigger cousins. When Daniel arrives I am going to set him to digging a latrine in the copse. His idea Harry. He said if we are living outdoors then we should do it properly. As he is the man of the house this week we will let him do that little job.

He has also mentioned shooting rabbits but I really didn't want to get any guns out of the shop that had not been sold. So have made cloth rabbits and filled them with rags. They have a big plastic target on the side of them so the suckers of the arrows will stick, I hope. I cut up some of the dresses you liked so much to see me wear, to make the rabbits and stuffed them with more of those frocks. So we have the only flowered rabbits in the country. I hope it works. I did try it out and if the rabbits are tied to a stake in the ground then we can see if the arrows will stick. I also made a big brown sheep out of my mink coat, the one that you said gave us status. I hated that coat. They can shoot it.

What a waste, you had very poor taste Paula, that mink cost a fortune and if only you had the presence to carry it off.

69

Unfortunately you looked like a trussed up sheep in it yourself. A coat like that should be worn with grace and style. Oh well, another waste of effort on my part to make you into something.

Wednesday 4th August.

Time for the children to go home.

'I am going to have to hose you down before you come indoors, Daniel,' Molly said, only half joking.

'Yes, I think these two can go straight into the bath as well,' Sandi said.

'They are all a bit mucky, but did you all have fun kids? Paula asked.

'Oh Grandma, it was great and we really must do it again. I like my own bedroom, but can we bring some friends with us as well?' Daniel asked.

'Well, it's okay with me if it's okay with your Mum and Dad,' Paula answered.

'Hmm well we will have to see,' Molly said.

'Blimey, if you think you can cope, Mum I'm all for it. How long do you think you can manage them? A week? Two?' Sandi enthused.

'John and Eric will be over later on when they leave off work to take all this lot down and tidy the garden for you, Mum.'

'Why don't we just put everything inside the big tent and leave it up for the summer. Then it will be ready at a moment's notice when the kids want to come?' Paula's idea appealed to Eric and John, it meant less to do this evening.

I have a lady coming over in the morning; she is going to be my cleaner. I have always hated housework, so now someone else can do it. I hate to admit that the house is dirty, well, I am sure she will clean it up for me. I haven't been bothered to do much of it. Mrs. Montgomery but she said to call her Mrs. M.

She said she loved doing housework, the muckier the better, when I spoke to her on the phone.

'Good,' I said, 'you will really enjoy yourself here. The place is filthy.'

We used to have a 'lady that does' when I was still working but you let her go when I retired from the warehouse. You asked why I would need help in the house when I had all this time on my hands now. You were very particular about how the house looked as well, you liked it just so. It meant I would spend at least five hours a day cleaning and then there was the washing and cooking, so I didn't have time to go out much, or write, or paint. Or for any of my hobbies in fact. We found time for yours though. Shooting and sailing.

Well, you are not here now, Harry, and I am going to have a cleaning lady. As far as I am concerned, cleaning the house does not count as living a life. Now I want more. I'm not sure I didn't always want more, and often said that to you. Your answer to that would be,

'Well, we could have some more babies.' I love the girls to distraction but no, I didn't want any more children.

I am beginning to see Harry, just how much of my life was put on hold, to boost yours. Maybe that's why I miss you so much. You not only put my life on hold for thirty two years but you took it and moulded it into yours. Now you are not here and I have to find my life again. Oh, I didn't tell you I have also joined a local art class, and a book club.

I have written a few poems as well so I am thinking of joining a writers circle also.

Well go ahead, if you think you have the talent. Poems? Painting? Writing? Well don't blame me when it all goes sadly wrong.

Thursday 5th August

I went riding again today in my new jodhpurs. I also stayed on to help with the horses and regain some of my stable management experience. I love it, being back with horses, I feel so alive. I am beginning to dislike coming home. The house is so empty without you Harry. It is not a comfortable place to be, your presence filled the house and filled my life. Half of it has gone now and I am finding the house oppressive.

I'm still here Paula, every time you think of me I'm still here in your head.

I have an appointment with our solicitor tomorrow, He has been finding out if there is any money left. He said it took a long while to locate all the accounts you had and to ascertain how much, if any there was in each. He should have all the information tomorrow. Will you have left me enough to live on? I know you had that retirement fund but I also know you liked spending.

I didn't take much notice of money. I know I had my earnings all invested and you knew where that was so I left all that side of things to you. I don't know how much I have and where it is. You handled it so well, and just told me what I could spend, if I wanted to. So I don't know really if I need to look for another job? You always said that I shouldn't worry about it and that you would see us right. Let's face it Harry, you had big plans for your retirement, so I am hoping you budgeted for it.

It was none of your business how much money was in those accounts. All you needed was what I gave you for housekeeping and your pin money. Now I suppose you will find out, nothing I can do about that now. I no longer have control.

I have been spending quite a bit since you left us. New clothes for a start, but as I have decided your car is more comfortable I have sold mine. And I have taken all your guns to the gunsmith place in town. I finally found the key to the cabinet in your desk drawer. They said they would sell them for me. You spent a lot of money on those guns Harry. Some of them are apparently very valuable. Your yacht and dinghy are both up for sale as well. Blimey, I could buy a house with what they cost.

Talking of houses, I had a sneaky peek at some houses online today. A nice house or bungalow, with maybe three bedrooms for when the children want to come and stay. Closer to the town, so I have some neighbours to call on if there is a need. And some company. Something newer, so there is not much maintenance. This house was your dream and we spent a good deal of time, energy and money on it over the years It was a wreck when we first moved in and we have done loads to it.

Do you remember camping out in the kitchen while we worked on the upstairs? Fun times though Harry, we enjoyed deciding what to do with it, although I would have always liked to take that wall out to make the kitchen bigger and have it all open plan you always said that we could do all that sort of stuff later, that for now all we had to do was make it comfortable. It was made comfortable but we never did the things we said we would do. It's as if having done it once, you lost interest. Temporary cheap furniture became permanent. In all these years we never replaced it. Then there is all this land and of course the copse.

When Daniel was only five and he wanted to go shooting in there? I was really scared. But you took him and showed him how to use my small gun. He still talks of it. I was really frightened he would hurt himself, or you. You know just how easily accidents can happen with guns, don't you Harry?

Friday 6th August

Well, that's a turn up for the books. Mr Fraser said that you had left me very well off. Rich in fact. You always said you would provide and you did. Thank you Harry, you really did look after me, well done my lovely man. All our hard work has paid off, for me it has. You Harry won't be able to have the pleasure of it. It didn't seem to bring you much happiness while you were alive either. If you were enjoying life, why would you have drunk so much all the time? And why would you have a need for those condoms I found in your suit pocket? Some questions will never be answered will they Harry?

'In the terms of Harry's will, you have been left a considerable lump sum. He has not mentioned all the other accounts that were in his own name but as his wife you will also inherit the funds in those. We still need to ascertain exactly how much that would be. As you know both of your wills were taken out at the same time and because it was advantageous tax wise for each to leave your assets to each other that is how they were set out.

Harry however added a codicil to his will about five years ago. In this he stated that he wanted the house to be transferred into the ownership of your daughters in equal proportions. He stated that you should be able to continue to live there until such time as you began another relationship or remarried. He left his shares in the business to your daughters and yourself equally. This may lead to some capital gains tax liability to your daughters. Do you wish to carry on with the mortgage Harry used to buy the house in town with?' Mr Fraser asked.

'How embarrassing, Mr Fraser, I know nothing of a mortgage. Or a house in town. Where is it?'

'Well, £536.24 each month is being paid out of one of Harry's accounts for a house. Number 7 Charter Avenue. It has a tenant who is paying a nominal rent.'

Paula admitted that she knew nothing about it and Mr Fraser went very red. She asked how long these payments had been made for and he said he would look closer into it. He gave Paula a knowing look which said a lot more.

As she left the solicitor's office Paula, was full of questions, but Mr Fraser had indicated that we wanted to investigate more before he talked to her about it.

Having finished her interview with Mr Fraser, Pauline decided she would browse the estate agents window she spied a bungalow that took her fancy. Now she knew she could afford to live wherever she wanted she went in to enquire about it. She made an appointment to view. Tomorrow, which is really quite quick.

There was plenty in the lump sum to buy a house and give the farm house to the girls, and still have a good income from her shares in the business and the other investments Harry had. And her own pension which would mature when she turned sixty.

Saturday 7th August.

Well I have just come back from viewing the bungalow, Harry and I love it. It will need a lot of work but that can be done before I move in this time. It is in a lovely spot, just on the edge of the town, five minutes' walk from the beach.

It was built in the seventies and really not had much done to it since by the looks of it. It has three bed rooms a big lounge, diner and with a wall out I can incorporate the kitchen as well. Really open plan. There is a nice little room I can make into an office, studio, writing room. A big family bathroom and an ensuite to the master bedroom. In a quiet road but with neighbours either side. Not a very big garden but big enough to put the tent up and for the children to have fun. I love it.

Not a bad price as far as I can see but I think I will put a cheeky offer in. As a cash buyer I may be able to grab a bargain.

Be careful Paula, do you really know what you are doing? You are very innocent in these things and without me to guide you will make a big mistake.

Sunday 8th August

Paula had spent most of the night researching things to do around the bungalow. She knew she would need to make some new friends if she did go there.

It's funny how most our friends seem to have disappeared in the mists of time. I wonder why that is? Maybe they were never my friends, just yours. Maybe they are afraid of the new rich widow, does a single woman of a certain age pose a threat? I am sad about some of them not keeping in touch. Maybe they are just leaving me to grieve. That would make sense. Death is still one of those subjects that people find hard to talk about.

There is a book club quite local to the bungalow, she thought she could join, writers circle as well. Art groups. And of course there is always the W.I.

You always used to laugh about them, didn't you Harry. You called them the Wandering Idiots. Yes, I like it more and more. I will ring tomorrow and make an offer. I will sell this house, Harry, leave it behind, along with its sixteen acres and copse. The girls are welcome to it.
I am going to leave behind our thirty two years and I am going to leave you behind, Harry.

I will always be with you inside your head Paula, guiding you, making sure you do nothing stupid. You will not be able to manage without me there to tell you what to do. That's not supposed to happen, I can keep a look out for you if you stay here but not when you leave the house.

77

I'm sorry that you can't enjoy the fruits of our labours Harry. I still feel it is such a shame. All the plans you had for your retirement for us to sail around the coast, to go clay pigeon shooting. All those things you were looking forward to. I have no desire to ever shoot a gun again and I never did enjoy the sailing. I was often sick when we were on the yacht and especially if we went out to sea. You said I would get used to it, and that it was mind over matter. All in my head, you said. Sometimes I wondered if you were truly blind to me, or just selfish. You were probably right, I would have got used to it, but now I don't have to. I don't have to do anything I don't want to do just because you wanted to do them. I can go do the things I like to do.

Oh, by the way, the bungalow is less than a mile away from the stables, the ones where I will be keeping the horse I am going to buy. The girls don't know about the bungalow yet. I will make sure I can have it first.

Bloody horses!

Monday 9th August
I just phoned the estate agent and put an offer in on the bungalow. Now I wait.

'So how did you get on with Mr Fraser the other day then Mum?

'Very interesting. I have to talk to you both about his will shall we meet up at the weekend?'

'How about Sunday lunch at ours then, Eric wants to get the barbecue out and we can only hope the weather stays good enough to eat outside.'

'Sounds good, what time?'

'Well come over whenever you like but we should eat about 1 o'clock. I'll ring Sandi and let her know.'
Molly rang back and said she had spoken to Sandi but they were going to John's Mums for Sunday lunch.
Paula said. 'How about tea here on Saturday then? I think Sandi said she was free Saturday. I'll ring her and check but I'm sure the kids would enjoy a pic-nic in the garden. I'm getting quite good at making cakes and things now.'

'Yes, that's fine. After Daniel gets back from his footy training.'

'Sandi, are you free for Saturday tea? I know you are going to John's Mums Sunday?'

'Oh good the girls were just saying it's about time to come over to yours again. Lovely we will pop over about 4 o'clock then.'

Tuesday 10th August.

I received a phone call from the estate agent. The offer has, she said, reluctantly been accepted, as long as we can complete within a month. It's empty of people even though it's still fully furnished. Apparently the gentleman who lived there died and the children want it sold quickly. Mr Fraser has said it would be possible, a push, but possible. So I have started the process of buying my first home without you Harry.
I need to talk to the girls now.

Paula went into town to have a look at the house Harry has been paying for. It's a nice little house, between the wars three bed roomed semi-detached in a pleasant road. In good condition and well maintained by the looks of it. Not a cheap getaway but a family home. Why would Harry want such a place and only charge a nominal rent? Mr Fraser had told Paula that in his opinion Harry could have got much more from his investment.

I saw her there, that same woman, just coming out with the child. So you didn't always use the condoms then, did you Harry? She saw me, and just looked. I drove off.

No Paula. At least she gave me a son. Something you couldn't or wouldn't do. Oh I know it's all down to the man but if you would have produced more children for me we could have had a son eventually.

Saturday 14th August.

Tea time with the family. Homemade cakes and scones, jellies and jam. You used to do the baking but I am getting a bit better at it now. We can have this picnic outside today because it isn't raining and has been dry for a few days. I have got all the new toys out and bought a big paddling pool for the kids. It has a slide in it and I have got that tarpaulin out with the hose again. It will be a fun day. I will walk down to the copse and see how your tree is Harry, and see if you are still there. I feel you less now I think you have moved on. Time for me to do the same.

You may go away from here Paula but you will never truly move on. I will always be with you. Anyway I'm not sure it will be so easy for you to sell up with that covenant in my will. It's not your house to sell, it never was your house, it was mine and I always had control of it.

'I have to tell you something girls,' Paula said as they are walking in from the copse. She explained about the codicil in Harry's will and how Mr Fraser thought this may affect them.

'I want to sell this house. I've seen a bungalow in town and when it had been refurbished I will be able to move in. But this house, of course is yours now anyway.'

Molly stopped and stared at the house for a while, remembering her happy childhood here. Sandi just looked at her. She said, 'Well, that makes sense I suppose. It's really too big for one person and so is this garden,' she sighed.

'Are you sure Mum? You don't have to move out just because it isn't yours any more,' Molly said.

'It never was mine anyway I never had my name on the deeds, it belonged to your father as he was often reminding me whenever he was angry with me. How can I go on living here now, without your dad? It's too big, too old, needs too much work to keep it right. I can't do it. You have moved on and are making your own memories, you don't need the house and garden to remember your times here. And the copse. How am I supposed to carry on living here knowing that is where your dad breathed his last? I can't do it. I need to get away from here.'

'It's very soon to be making decisions like that, that's all I mean. Don't go on Mum. I just think you are jumping too soon.'

'How long does it take, then Molly? You tell me. I hate being here without Dad. It's so lonely, so sad and I can't get over him while I am still here.'

'Over him? He was your husband, how can you get over him?'

'Molly, don't be obtuse, I will grieve for your father till the day I die, and you know very well I will. But, I kind of hope that will be a few years away and that I will be able to have another life before then. Oh, don't worry I don't think I will ever get married again. No one will replace your dad. Anyway, one marriage was quite enough, thank you. I have had enough of doing whatever other people want me to do and like it or not I am now going to do whatever **I** want to do.'

'Fine, if that's what you want. You do that, Mum, you do just what you want,' Molly walked off indoors.

Sandi said, 'Don't worry Mum, she'll come round and we will find a way to sort that little problem out. Molly just doesn't like change.'

'She liked change well enough when she married Eric. But then it was her decision to move out and get married. We didn't give her a load of arguments about it.'

'I know, and she will see your point though, she just needs to see the practicality of it all. Of course you can't cope with this huge house on your own. It's ridiculous to think you should stay here anyway at your age.'

'Oi, I'm not that old.'

Sandi laughed, 'That's better. Oh here she comes.'

'We'll be off now Mum, thanks for tea, and everything.'

A quick peck on the cheek and she has gone.

Oh well, thought Paula. It is not Molly's choice where I live.

How very strange of you Harry.

You obviously either wanted me to stay here but at the will of our daughters and under their control or you were trying to get me out. Did you think that without you here to control me I would just let that control pass to the girls? Molly takes after you in that aspect, she tries to control everything around her and apparently that includes me as well. Or was it to see me gone from your precious house?

Paula thought that if she was to stay in the house but wanted to make it more comfortable she would have to ask permission from the girls for their approval of any alterations she wanted to be done. Therefore control of how she lived would indeed, in part be in the girls hands. But it seemed she was being forced out of the house. Because with the passing of some of the company shares and half of the house both the girls would be liable for capital gains tax. How would they have found that money? So the sale of the house seemed even more important now. Molly didn't like it but it would seem to be the only thing possible under the circumstances.

Paula, you surprised me there. I most certainly do not want another man in there to take my place in my house. I must admit I didn't think you had it in you to move on, I thought you would stay and just do as you were told. You have always been so compliant and weak. Am I losing my control over you? I don't like it one little bit.

Sunday 15th August

When Molly phoned she was quite apologetic and said it had been a shock. If I really wanted this she would not put up any objections, but had I really thought about it properly? After all, this has been my home for a lot of years. She supposed she had better come and have a look at this bungalow I was talking about buying before I did anything silly. I said I had already bought the bungalow and it is what I want. There was a long silence and I had the feeling Eric was standing next her. She sighed and said, 'Okay, you seem to have made your mind up.'

Oh she is your daughter alright Harry, but I am stronger now and will not let her bully me. Molly will come round in her own good time, but she is not coming to see my bungalow until I am ready to move in, I have decided that much.

Had Harry really thought that Paula would just stay in the house and be at the beck and call of the girls? Paula was totally confused about Harry's wishes. It was more likely that he was trying to continue to control her life from his after-life. He would not have expected her to move on from his precious house. He had not the faintest idea that Paula would have preferred it if they had not been quite so isolated and had near neighbours. That they could pop out for a pint of milk without having to get in the car. Yes the village was only two miles away. But carrying shopping it was quite a trek. To live in this big house alone would have made Paula uncomfortable and feel vulnerable.

Is that what he had wanted? Or as Paula suspected had he actually wanted her out? Did he love the house more than he loved her? It would seem as if he did because he was making all the moves to get rid of her.

Monday 16t^h August

Paula telephoned the estate agents and asked them to come round and value the house. They would need a value in any case so that the girls would have some idea of their inheritance.

I am going riding after the agent has been Harry. I am also going to have a look at a horse I may buy. I'm excited about that. He is a big round cob, with lots of hair. I may be too busy to write in this diary much but don't worry I haven't forgotten you. Now that I know I don't have to stay here I am not missing you so much and I don't feel your presence as often as I did. I sleep well now and don't need a couple of glasses of wine to send me off. I am in good health and feeling much more positive about what life without you holds for me.

Wednesday 1st September.

Paula had a phone call from Mr Fraser's office.

Things are progressing well with the purchase of the bungalow. He would need her to pop in and sign some papers. She informed him that she would not be moving in straight away but would be having extensive work done to it first. He knew of an architect friend who would be able to go round and have a look for her. Could he meet Paula there after we had completed and she could tell him what ideas she had for the place?

Mr Fraser said that as soon as we completed, he would give his friend my number.

Paula needed to discuss what she could do about the will. Would she be able to sell the house and give the money to the girls? Or should she just move out and give the whole house to them and let them sell it? She told him that it was in the process of being valued so at least they would know what amount they were talking about.

Mr Fraser said he would look into it and see what kind of tax implications there would be for the girls either way. He said that alternatively, Paula could spend some money on it and stay there.

See, Harry what a nuisance you have been? All because you were still trying to control me from beyond the grave. Now we have all this to go through, but if you thought that would make me stay here you have another think coming.

Did you think life would be easy without me there to tell you how to live it? You will mess up and you know it.

Thursday 2nd September
The little ones go back to school today. It always seems odd to me that school term starts on a Thursday, why not

just wait till the following Monday? But today they go. We have had a glorious summer together.

Whenever I have been home I invited them over and we played games in the garden. I found that old croquet set and brought it down from the attic. We had tournaments. Also badminton and the paddling pool was upgraded to a much bigger one which is more like a swimming pool. In fact Sandi and John came over quite a lot with Zoe and Dee and John taught them to swim in it. Daniel and Rachel have been over as well and Eric came often but I haven't seen that much of Molly. I think she is still sulking a bit.

Sandi says she will get over it. I'm afraid she will have to, the deed is done. I complete on the bungalow really soon. Well done Mr Fraser or your office anyway. So the bungalow is soon to be empty. I will speak with the architect to do some calculations and drawings. It looks very much as if I can have it exactly as I visualised it when I first went to look. I have found a garden design firm who will re-do the whole of the back garden as well. I didn't know I was so capable.

I have never taken control before, I left it all to you Harry. In doing so I had to have things to your liking. I don't think I had much input. Curtains, bedding, furniture even the saucepans were your choice. I just used them.

I'm not saying I didn't like them, I just didn't get to have a choice. So a-shopping I will go. I will go alone as well, I don't want anyone telling me what to have. It will be of my own choosing. If I make a mistake? Well, I will have to rectify it myself. It's not as if I can't afford a few mistakes. Nothing is forever Harry. How funny that I have started saying that again. It was always my refrain when I was young.

Oh you will make plenty of mistakes Paula. I never intended to let life without me easy for you, or you wouldn't miss me as you should. I wanted it to be easy for me, you were a secondary thought.

Friday 10th September

Well, we have completed and only a little over time but the deed is done. I saw Mr Fraser's friend the architect and he will be doing some calculations to give to the builders.

I really can't understand how you would prefer that hermetically sealed box you lovingly call a bungalow to my beautiful house. When I retired I was going to take you away for a few months and we would have come back to the house all revamped. I had plans for it. I know you would have liked it, I would have anyway. I have spent many an hour drawing plans up. It would have all been done just how I always wanted it.

Monday 13th September

By the time I have sifted through all the stuff in the attic I can't see that there will be much to store at the new house Harry I have brought it all down and put it in the lounge and dining room. Sandi has claimed the blanket chest as I knew she would and the grandfather clock as she has high ceilings. Molly has at last come round and looked through your jewellery and chosen your signet ring, gold fob watch and some gold chains. She said she had thought about some of the furniture but on closer inspection she realised it was not that good a quality.

Well we did buy most of it when we first married, didn't we Harry. When we didn't have much money.

'Yeah, dump it Mum, it's only so much rubbish. But can I have Dad's desk out of his study? That is a quality piece of furniture.'

'Of course you can. I won't have a use for it, I am having a fitted study built in.'

I wonder if it occurred to her that the only quality piece of furniture we ever bought was for your sole use Harry? I found all those plans in your desk drawer. The ones you had for the house here.

You were going to cut the kitchen in two and have it smaller with the dining table in the other half of the room. Then take down the wall between the dining room and the lounge to make that twice the size. That Harry would have isolated the kitchen and whoever was cooking would of necessity be alone in there as there would not have been room for two people while one was cooking.

Is that where you saw me Harry, in the kitchen on my own? Being more of a servant to you than I ever was. Never a partner? Never an equal?

Or sometimes I wanted to be alone in the kitchen without your inane chatter which had no substance, you had become really rather dim and I could almost say of no intelligence at all. You told me once that your life was so dull. How could you find life dull my dear? You had this lovely house to keep clean and the garden to keep tidy, you always had so much to do I made sure of that. I spent most of my life keeping you busy that should be enough for you.

I had a strange phone call today, not quite heavy breathing but silence. Wrong number? Maybe, I don't know and certainly I am not going to let it bother me.
I phoned Mr Fraser to see if he had found out anything about that house. I made an appointment to go and see him tomorrow.

Tuesday 14th September
Paula's appointment with Mr Fraser was at 3 o'clock. When she went into his office she saw quite a lot of official looking paperwork on his desk. He informed her that the mortgage Harry had taken on Charter Avenue was now nine years into a ten year mortgage.

Why a mortgage Harry? Did you think I would notice a large amount going out of one of your accounts? I don't know how I would have done as you controlled all the money and never let me look at the accounts. I didn't even know the prices of houses nine years ago.

Mr Fraser thought maybe it was an investment for the future. It will be all paid up by this time next year. Did she want to carry on with it? The house is worth much more now than when it was bought.
   Paula said she would have to think about it. She would be certain to let him know but there really didn't see any point in giving up on the payments when they were so close to finishing it.

Nine years ago Harry? That boy looked about eight years old. Is he your son as I suspected?

Again Paula drove to Charter Avenue and sat in the car looking at the house. She spied the woman walking along the street to the house and watched her go indoors.

The woman looked smart, slim, long blonde hair, in fact quite pretty. She was dressed in modern fashion as well.

In fact if I think about it she looks quite a lot like me when I was in my twenties before, I put on all that weight. The weight that you said suited me. The weight that meant I could not wear fashionable clothes and look good. So I wore the clothes you chose for me that hid the lumps and bumps. I also cut my hair because you said you liked it shorter, and let the grey bits show because you wanted me to grow old gracefully along with you.

Strange, how you never got any fatter Harry. You always kept your fine figure. You wore your suits fitted and looked smart for work and your jeans and weekend shirts made you look like a latter day James Bond, all expensive, and very good tailoring.

Wednesday 15th September
Well I am not going to think about all that right now Harry. I am going riding again. I have to have a look at the livery yard that is attached to the riding stables. There are lots of women of all ages who keep their horses there. It is a nice place and I have been getting to know them.

91

They are very friendly and helpful and when I buy my horse I know I will have lots of help and advice from them. Things have changed when it comes to looking after horses. And we sit and chat when all the work is done, those that don't have to rush off to work that is.

I was chatting to one girl, who was telling me about her friend who was very sad. Her boyfriend had been killed in a freak accident.

'Oh dear, that is terrible.'

'Yes, and her son's really upset. He, the boyfriend, worked away and the son didn't see much of him but he is going to be fatherless now.'

'How awful. Is she local?'

'Yes, she lives in town. He had bought a house and everything and was going to move in with her in a couple of years when he retired.'

'Retired? He must have been a good deal older than her then.'

'Yeah, in his fifties I think.'

'Oh, how sad.' Was all I could manage. I was finding it hard to breath Harry. I was having my suspicions about that woman and child, slowly being confirmed by the existence of the house but to hear the other side of the story was quite a shock.

Luckily some other girls came over and the subject was changed before I could start asking questions. But I do need to investigate all this Harry. You have had another woman on the go, which looks just like the one you said you fell in love with at first sight. Have I been so blind? I actually let you live exactly how you wanted to and in fact have two lives. I have been your servant, and let you dictate to me how I have lived. I had even let you take charge of how I looked. I became exactly what you wanted and so you went out and found a new, younger version. Would you have moulded her into a frump as well Harry? Or was she so much stronger in character than me?

When I had finished at the stables and booked a place for me when I got my horse, I went home to shower and change. I dressed with care but not too fashionably, I didn't want to be as you would put it, 'mutton dressed as lamb.' I wore a nice pair of jeans and a silk blouse with a fitted jacket. I combed my hair which is getting quite long but still grey. Then I got in your car and drove to the house. I sat outside for quite some time. I had to build up some reserves of inner strength.

I actually went for a walk around the neighbourhood to calm my nerves. I went back to the house and could see her in the front room. I opened the gate and walked up the path. The front garden looked very tidy and just how you would have liked to see it Harry. I suspected that you had laid it out and kept it tidy with the grass nicely cut and the edges all neatly trimmed.

As I waited on the doorstep for her to answer the door I was shaking. It took her a long while to come to the door and I was just about to give up when I saw the curtains twitch. She was obviously debating with herself whether to open the door and let me into her life.
She did open the door and looked very scared herself.

'Paula,' she said. Holding onto the door for dear life.

'There you have the advantage over me. I don't know your name.'

'Sharon.'

'Well Sharon, you had better let me in we have things to talk about.'

She held open the door for me to enter.

I had a good look around. It helped me to think what I was going to say to her I also hoped it would intimidate her. I was not in the mood to be particularly nice to her. She had been in the process of stealing my husband. Oh yes, I did recognise her from the funeral, and the other times I had seen her. She led the way into the lounge, where I sat and stared at her. Poor girl was shaking with fear.

'What did he promise you?'

She sat down in an exhausted heap. 'That we would be together when he retired, that he would be able to spend more time with me then and we would be happy.'

'What had he told you about me? That I didn't understand him? That I was fat and dowdy? That we had lived separate lives for years?'

She nodded. 'All of that and more. How you wouldn't go out with him, would never go abroad on holiday. You were a home maker and a boring housewife.'

'He didn't tell you that until a few years ago I was working in the business alongside him as well as bringing up two children and running a household? Going shooting with him, going sailing with him, how I wanted to go abroad but he wouldn't? How we slaved to build a business just as he wanted us to? How I put my life on hold so that he could achieve his ambitions? Did he tell you any of those things?'

She shook her head. I have to admit I felt sorry for her, but I wasn't about to let her know that, I was just building up a good steam of anger, not towards her so much Harry but towards you. You, Fucking shit-head.

'What are you going to do?'

'Nothing right now, I have to think about this. I have only just found out who you are.'

She looked at the clock and I knew she had to get to the school to pick up her son, your son, Harry.

'What's he called? *Your* son.'

'Jake.'

'I'll go now and you can get him, but I will be in touch, somehow, although I never want to see you again.'

I got up and walked out. I sat in the car shaking with shock, rage and oh I don't know what.

So now you have met her, for all the good it did for you. She is very similar to the young you that much I do have to admit. But she won't let me dictate to her. She is her own woman even though she does take full advantage of what I have to offer. Financially and physically. Yes she is part of the reason I spend so many nights in my recliner chair, for one thing I was too tired to come to bed and let's face it Paula, why would I want to spend the night in the same bed as you when I could have stayed with Sharon?

I went to Molly's.

'Did you know?' I asked her as I walked in the house.

'Not until recently.' Funny how she knew what I was talking about isn't it Harry?

'About the child?'

'He's at the same school as Rachel, a year younger. He told her about his father and Eric and I sussed it out.'

'Were you ever going to tell me?'

'I don't know Mum. How did you find out?'

'Mortgage payments from one of your father's accounts.' I was totally deflated and exhausted. I got up to go home. Molly didn't try to stop me.

Paula drove home on automatic pilot. She was not thinking of where she was going and only realised she was home when she stopped at the automatic gate waiting for it to open. She went indoors and walked straight up the stairs. Fully clothed, she lay on the bed and fell into an exhausted sleep.

She woke at two in the morning and went down stairs to make herself a cup of tea. She just couldn't believe that she had been quite so gullible and had really not noticed that Harry had a second life. How she had believed him when he had told her he was at work.

She had even still been working at the main warehouse in the head office while he was starting his affair and having a child with that woman. How could that be? He often said he had meetings with new business contacts and there was no doubt he brought in plenty of business but how when he was obviously spending so much time with her? Well Sharon had known about is proper family so he didn't have to hide his first life from his second at least but he did hide his second life from his first very successfully.

SHIT, SHIT. SHIT. Harry. You bastard!

Thursday 16th September
That feeling of dread is back again Harry. It's like grieving all over again. How could you have been so

duplicitous all these years? How far down had I fallen to not be able to see what you were doing?

Paula got all the bank records out and looked to see if Harry had actually provided for his son. After some hours of looking at all the different accounts she found a payment of £15,000 a year into an account. She then looked under 'S' in the little black address book and found a number which may have been Sharon's. Only one way to find out, she thought and rang the number. Yes, it was her number. Paula asked her if Harry had been putting money into an account for Jake. Yes, she said there was a trust fund for him.

'Good,' she said and put the phone down. Well Harry had provided for him. Now, what to do about the house? Let her stay there? She phoned Mr Fraser's office and asked for him to ring her back.

'The Charter Avenue house? Is that solely in Harry's name? She asked him.

'Yes indeed it is his is the only name on the deeds. It is now your house.'

Yes it's mine. But I still don't know what to do. She thought.

Both Sandi and Molly arrived together. Sandi had been told all about it and they came to see what they could do.

'We are as shocked as you are, Mum. How could it have happened?

'How could Dad have another child when he was hardly away from your side?' Sandi asked.

'Hardly away?' come on Sandi he was always sliding off. Okay I grant you he always came home each night but in the last few years he was more often at work than

97

at home. And even when we still lived here sometimes he wouldn't get home from work till after we had all gone to bed,' Molly scoffed.

'But he didn't stay away, did he? He was always here for breakfast in the morning.'

'Not for the last few or so years and especially since I retired he often was up and out before I got up.' I told them. 'Perhaps he hadn't even been home. We had been rather distant and he was more into doing his own thing. He told me that it was all for our good and when he retired we could spend much more time together. That we had the rest of our lives to enjoy our time together. Was he planning on leaving me and going to her when he finally retired? Was that the great plan? Did he plan to take her sailing round the coast?

How would he have coped with Jake? He didn't have all that much time for your kids, but then again I suppose this one is your brother. He told her that he would be with her when he gave up work that they would be together.'

'Well, I do hesitate to say it Mum, but you had rather let yourself go,' Molly says.

Paula gasped at the unfairness of this.

'Right, let me tell you something. Your oh-so-perfect father chose my clothes, he chose my weight, he chose my activities, he chose my reading matter, he chose my house, my decoration, my friends, not that I seem to still have many of those, he dictated about how I spent my day. Why do you think I had no cleaning lady when I retired? He decided I could do all the cleaning as I now had all day with nothing to do. He chose my car, he chose what I watched on the television, and the music we had in the house. He lived my life for me and now I find he has betrayed me.'

Paula realised she was shouting this tirade and had been stomping around the kitchen and thumping her fist on to the table top. She stopped and looked at their faces and added

'And my hair style.'

Then I started laughing, although a bit hysterically. The girls were shocked at the tirade and really didn't know what to say.

Finally Sandi said, 'Bloody hell he really was a control freak, wasn't he? Is this why you waited so long to go back to horse riding? You said you were going to have a horse again one day. Wouldn't Dad let you have one?'
I had to sit down again.

'He was never so blatant, he obviously didn't want me to, so he filled my days with activities that he wanted me to do so that there was no time left. I see that now. I waited until you were grown before I mentioned it as neither of you had shown any inclination towards it. When you had both gone I thought the time was right but he had other ideas. I thought it was because he was still working so hard and trying to make us rich, I felt rather guilty about how much time he was at work so never pushed it too much. So we went shooting and sailing. Now I find that he wasn't working all God's hours he was procreating with another woman.'

'I feel so let down, such a fool,' I was crying tears of frustration. Feeling the hysteria rising. You fucking bastard Harry.

'No, Mum, he lied to you all these years and to her as well. He would never have left this house to go and live with her. He wasn't tolerant of children so much as he got older, he would have been driven crazy having a child under his feet all day long. He wouldn't have gone anywhere but would've kept you both on a string. I can see that now. It all falls into place,' Sandi told me.

'Yes, sometimes when he has obviously told you that he was at work, Eric would say that he had left early,' Molly added.

'Hmm, so now we know where he was. I suppose there is only one mistress?'

'Oh God.' Both the girls groaned at that.

'So what to do? That house is yours.'

'I don't know. I can't kick the kid out can I? None of this is his fault. I'll speak with Mr Fraser to see what can be done legally but I think she has to stay there. Does she work? Or was he keeping her? I didn't see any evidence of payments to her in his accounts, just the trust fund for the boy.'

'Well, if she isn't she will just have to get a job now, won't she? I don't see why you should keep her *and* the kid.'

I am tired again now Harry. Oh goodness you have caused some problems and I have to deal with them. At least both girls are talking to me now, so that is a blessing. I thought I had got a bit further than bursting into uncontrollable tears but I find I am crying a lot again. You did this to me Harry. You fucking did this to me.

Oh Paula, you were so easy to deceive. That is your problem, you always saw the best in people, me included and never looked past what you were told. You believed everything without question. So easy, so very easy.

I think I need to go back to the doctor, I can feel the hysteria rising. Perhaps he can recommend someone to give me some counselling. I am feeling really low again.

I will go see Mr Fraser and tell him I will pay off the mortgage, Sharon and Jake can stay there until he is out of education but she must pay the market rent and I will stop the payments going into the trust fund. I am not paying for your bastard Harry. I expect he will be in line to receive it when he is eighteen but I don't know and I'm really not that bothered.

Mr Fraser can write to her with these terms and that's that, as far as I am concerned. I want never to see or hear from them again.

Yes, that is my decision. I think that is pretty fair.

Friday 17th September.

Paula woke with the familiar feeling of dread, even though this was supposed to be a happy day, the day to view the horse she planned to buy. It would involve riding him after she had watched him being ridden. If she liked him she would have the vet out to check him over before she bought him and possibly go and ride him a few times, just so they could get to know each other.

Then she had an appointment with a builder at the bungalow. She had already spoken with the architect friend of Mr Fraser's and plans were in the process of being drawn up for the alterations Paula wanted.

101

Whichever builders she chose would have a good set of plans to work from but she wanted a ball park figure of costs before she decided exactly how she wanted it to be.

First the horse.

Well I loved him, straight away. I had a ride in the ménage and then we went out for a hack. He is a little bit nervous of large traffic like trucks and tractors but nothing I can't handle and not in any way dangerous.

He has lovely paces not like a pony but nice long strides. He is fifteen hands high and a big round fellow. He is called Nicholas. I have paid a deposit so no one else can come and steal him away from me and I will go and see him and ride lots over the next month. That's when the stable becomes available. I will have to arrange transport. Buy him a saddle, and arrange a saddle fitter to come to see him as soon as I get him settled. Oh I am so excited.

I need to get some feed in that he has and oh there are lots of things to buy. I will have some happy hours online getting stuff in for him. He will have all brand new things. He is five years old so, a good age. Sod you Harry, I am starting my new life. Right now! I am still so angry with you that I am not even sorry that you are missing this new me. But thinking about, it this new me is the old me, the one you fell in love with. Did you ever really love me Harry? Or did you just need someone to control?

Paula, you are the mother of two of my children. As such of course I loved you. Sharon was just a convenience to me she filled the space that you left empty because you had become so unattractive. And she gave me a son. Don't forget that little fact. I had to keep some control over you I couldn't face the thought that someone else would find you attractive and lure you away from me.

Tuesday 21st September.

I had to be up really early today Harry, as I am driving to the airport to catch a flight. And I am going all alone.

You know I said about joining social media sites? Well, one of the girls I use to go to college with got in touch with me. That is the college that I left to marry you Harry. She lives in Greece and she has invited me to go and visit her. The lack of sleep doesn't matter really, as I am so excited and a bit worried at the same time. This is something I have never done before Harry. Last time I went abroad was with my parents. We never went, did we?

As soon as Jenny got in touch with me she said, 'Finally escaped him then?' I told her what had happened and she was sorry that you had died and joked that there were easier ways to get rid of you.

Skype. It's a wonderful tool Harry I don't know why I didn't find it before. We had long conversations over the airwaves and caught up on our lives since I last saw her.

So we fixed a date for me to go and I looked online for flights. They fly on Tuesdays. The flight is six, thirty five in the morning so I need to be at the airport by half past four which I have looked up and is a two hour drive. I think I will leave the house at about half past one in the morning, just in case I get lost and then won't panic about being late. I booked the flight, sorted out my new passport, booked parking, all online. Well, not the passport. I have even checked in and have my boarding pass.

Goodness this is exciting Harry. First time ever on my own. You always sorted out holidays and I just went wherever you decided. I can't say I didn't enjoy our holidays Harry. I loved spending time alone with you.

You could be so funny and endearing. I will feel at a bit of a loss without you I expect.

I arrived at the airport and was directed to zone E to park. There is a bus to take you to the terminal building. Just got to remember which zone I am in and the number of the bus stop. Through security with no problem and then I needed to find a coffee.

Gosh Harry, you would have moaned at the price. Nearly five pounds for a cup of coffee and a bottle of water. If you were here we would have taken flasks of tea and sandwiches. A nice gentleman helped me put my case in the overhead locker. You would have done that wouldn't you Harry? So at least that much is the same. I brought a book with me as it is a four hour flight and I thought I may get bored. But I was sitting by a window and as we climbed through the clouds Harry, I was enthralled. The beauty of the cloud bank, it looked as if you could walk on it. Big fluffy marshmallow mountains spread out below us.

Then as we flew south and the clouds broke up a bit I could see the white capped mountains that we flew over. It does make you feel very small Harry to be up here and look down on the huge swathes of green land, with lakes, forests, hills and rivers. We didn't seem to fly over many towns and cities, but from up here it was not easy to see them anyway. Then the sea, that looked like silver silk. So beautiful it took my breath away, Harry.

There was a bit of a commotion when one poor chap fainted. The flight crew laid him out flat with his feet up in the air and stayed with him till he woke up. He was alright but looked really pale as he sat back down. Poor chap. Maybe he had been really nervous.

Was that the real reason you didn't ever want to go abroad Harry? You were scared? I remember my mum flew to Australia on her own. My brother and I took her to the airport and we got caught in a traffic jam and we arrived at the check in desk at the time the flight was supposed to leave. The girl said that the flight had been delayed because the pilot was in the same traffic jam so she caught her flight.

So If Mum could do it, I thought I could as well Harry. I have amazed myself these last few months at just how much I can do alone. You would always arrange everything and all I had to do was pack the suitcases and get in the car. The rest was down to you.

At my age I am doing all these things for the first time, Harry and alone. I still wish you were here to see all these wondrous things. Like the cloud that looked exactly like a dolphin jumping out of the sea.

That is something I will always remember and think how beautiful nature is. We would sometimes lie in the garden watching clouds and trying to make objects out of them. Horses, chickens, cars and that time you said you saw the road runner from that cartoon. You won't ever experience this though Harry.

I pondered on the thought of how much of the experience you would notice. I glanced out of the window and saw another plane, going in the opposite direction. It looked as if it was going much faster than us.

I wondered if there was someone in that plane glancing out of their window thinking the same thing. Oh, the joys of the world. I am having the time of my life and it's just a shame you are not with me. I have almost forgiven you for Sharon and Jake

That's probably, because I am feeling so good about myself now. So liberated. Would I have been so forgiving if you were here Harry? I doubt it somehow. I would have boiled up inside with resentment. Would we have had rows about it or would I have just accepted the situation and let you get on with it? I expect I would have taken the easy way out, as I now realise I have always done. Let you have it all your way. Let you control my life and almost live it for me. How did that happen? How did this independent girl become so dependent?

Greece is a lovely place and Jenny met me at the airport in her white open top car. Another new experience Harry. I have never driven along the road with the wind in my hair. You always had the windows shut and the air conditioning on. That has decided me. I need to sell your car as well and buy a sports car. I really don't need a big car. If I take the children out, I can always borrow one of the girls' cars. Yes, something else to research. What sort of car do I want? What colour?

Jenny's house is superb. I don't know what I expected but it is a nice three bedroom modern house with a big garden. She has olive trees that are 160 years old. She never has to buy olive oil. We toured all around went shopping quite a lot as well and I thought I would have to buy a bigger case to get it all home.

But I didn't care, I was enjoying myself. We had such fun recounting our times at college. I had forgotten what fun I used to have and what a rascal I was. Not a care in the world Harry. It was the same when we first got together, we were so carefree. But it didn't take long for us to get into the work pattern. I am thankful for that now Harry as I am a wealthy woman and will never have to worry about money and where it will come from.

So you see, having money isn't everything. Even rich people can be poor. Unsatisfied. Unhappy. You must have been unsatisfied, Harry, or Sharon and Jake would not have been in your life. I still keep thinking about them and I still get angry sometimes.

What a lovely week I had. Jenny has invited me back again and I will definitely be going again. I have done it now, I am a seasoned traveller. I am finding more and more things I can do without you Harry.

When you first died I wondered how I would manage to live a life as one person and not half of two. But I am managing fine. In fact I like it. I don't think I will ever want to share it again, ever want to comply with someone else's wishes. I can do what I want, when I want.

You will never be able to live alone Paula, you will want someone else to direct you and guide you, believe me. You have done everything I wanted you to do for so long I am surprised you actually know how to make a decision without consulting the world and his wife first. You are just not capable of living on your own. But the trouble is my love who would want you? Not many that's for sure. I always told you that you were lucky to have me as no-one else would ever want you.

Wednesday 28th September

Did you have a good week away then Mum?' Molly asked when she phoned her mother. She felt she had to make sure Paula arrived home without incident.

'Yes, thank you it was absolutely marvellous,' I even managed to get myself to the airport and home again.'

'Sandi and I have been talking while you were away and we think that if you are determined you won't stay in the house any more we may as well sell it when you move. You did have a valuation done, didn't you?'

'Yes I did but they told me that it would have a limited market as it is so big and with so much land.'

'Oh good, thanks Mum, I'm glad you had a nice time, bet you have loads of photos to download. Daniel will come and help you with that.'

'Already done, and they are on their way to you, the ones I haven't already sent that is. But of course Daniel can come over any time he likes.'

'Shall we have some lunch one day this week? I expect you have a tan you want to show off?'

'Good idea, See you soon. Love you.'

Mrs. M. had been busy with the house while Paula was away and had cleaned it top to bottom. Paula thought she was in seventh heaven, she had always hated housework, and to have someone like Mrs. M. to do it was her idea of perfection.

She phoned the estate agent and told them to go ahead and market the house. She agreed a price with them and informed them who the vendors actually were. She was in two minds whether she should phone the girls and see if they were happy with the price but decided that she would forever be discussing it with them so decided she would take control of this project.

The agent was happy to deal with her but they would write to Molly and Sandi and inform them of Paula's involvement and have written proof that this was agreed by the girls. She could understand that they had to keep it right. So once all that was done and the brochure made the house would be up for sale.

Paula wondered if she should have a contingency plan if the house sold before the bungalow was ready for her to move into.

She smiled when she remembered her mother being quite sarcastic about a friend who was getting her house ready before she married and moved in.

'Susan is getting married in spring and she wants me to be her maid of honour,' Paula had told her. Her mother had answered.

'Oh, is her freezer full?'

Well, Paula thought I will have a full freezer before I move in to this house, Mum.

The agent reiterated that they would have a limited market as the house was so big and although it was beautiful and in a superb location it did need a lot of work

for a new family. Paula discussed the price and settled on one that seemed reasonable, she didn't want the girls to lose out but also didn't want it hanging around too long on the market.

She would have felt awful if the girls were faced with having to find the capital gains tax money before they had the cash from the house. The agent said she would market it maybe as a small holding or ripe for conversion as a Bed and Breakfast or even to use the land as pasture for ponies or alpacas.

Paula wondered if there would be a way to retain some of the land for the girls to keep and perhaps at a later date try for planning permission to build on it. Still that was for another day. Right now she had some research work to do as she wanted to buy a new car. So it was back to the internet and look to find a nice nippy little sports car.

Thursday 30th September

I am seeing the second of three builders round at the bungalow today who are going to give me a quote for the work I want done. They will have all had a set of plans to study by now and they may have ideas that I like as well. All recommended either by Sandi, or the architect or the double glazing firm who I have bought the windows from. That is the first thing that needed doing as the old ones were nearly as rotten as the ones here, Harry. The roof apparently is sound which is a bonus. Being a bungalow any walls I want removed can be done a bit easier, they tell me, unless I want to use the loft space as an attic room.

Paula said she would like to find a way to do it easily if anyone wanted to make those changes after her but for her own purposes she would not need a loft as such. She saw that there would be plenty of cupboard space and as she was downsizing in all senses of the word she would not have much left to put in the cupboards anyway.

110

This was becoming very exciting now and Paula couldn't believe that she was doing all this unaided. When she was young, she would have been able to see something like this through with no problem, but after all those years deferring to Harry's wishes she felt proud of herself and frightened at the same time. She knew that over the years she had let him take over her life and she also knew that she probably could have stopped it from happening. There had been some terrific arguments in the early years but after a while Paula found it was so much easier to just let him have his own way, It would save all the name calling. The insults. Him constantly telling her that she was lucky to have him and no one else would look at her.

When they were out together if she talked to another man he would call her a whore and say that he had saved her from herself when he married her. He always made it sound as if he had done her a favour by marrying her and that she would have been nothing without him. Then if she argued back he would sulk for weeks. Literally weeks, of not talking to her. Like the time he had come home from the village with some crispy rolls and cheddar cheese. He went out to the garden and picked three over-ripe tomatoes. Paula had always liked her tomatoes under ripe not squashy.

He said. 'We can have some nice cheese and tomato rolls for lunch.'

Paula said. 'Nice but I think I will have cheese and pickle in mine. That stuff I made the other week.' He asked her what was wrong with his tomatoes. Were they not good enough for her? She told him that just this one time she wanted pickle and was sure his tomatoes would be delicious.

But, she pointed out he had not even tried her pickle yet. He took offense that she didn't want his tomatoes. That sulk went on for two whole weeks. She would apologise in the end and tell him he was right and she would do as she was told because she just could not stand the atmosphere in the house. That's how it all started. Paula, losing her identity and becoming a shadow of Harry.

As the years went on it was just normal for Harry to decide everything and for her to comply. Not any longer. She had not forgotten how to make a decision. She was beginning to gain the confidence to do just that to plan her own life and the way she wanted to live it. She was getting stronger by the day and all the years of playing second fiddle to Harry were slipping away. Yes it was liberating but also very frightening, but she reasoned that if she made a mistake she would learn by it and then rectify it.

Monday 4th October.

Today is my birthday. The first time I have woken on my birthday alone for thirty two years. You would have made it special. Starting with breakfast in bed, no matter what else we were doing. I would get up, have a leisurely bath and then we would go out for the day.

Sometime during the day there would be a time window for the girls to visit. Today we are going into town as a threesome. Shopping and lunch. No riding today.

I turned up the heating last night, it was a bit chilly. I don't have to wear three cardigans to keep warm now Harry, I turn the knob. The whole house is warm. Molly and Sandi are coming to pick me up at about 10 o'clock. Molly will drive us into town so I can have a glass of wine with my lunch. We are going to the new Italian restaurant. I love continental food.

You would always take us to a pub for steak and chips or a roast. Very nice and I always had lovely meals usually followed by both our puddings. You never ate yours and it seemed silly to let them go to waste. Today we are having Italian. I have been to the hairdressers and had my hair restyled, how you would have hated it. I told the girl I was growing it long so she gave me a style that will grow out nicely and not look untidy while it is growing. She said to come back every six weeks to have a smidgeon trimmed off to keep it right.

'Shouldn't you turn the heating down while we're out Mum?' Molly asked her just before they left.
I pondered on this for nearly a second as Harry would have turned it down before they left, but then she said

'No, I'll leave it, and then it'll be warm to come home to.'
Sandi smiled. 'You little rebel you.'
What a lovely birthday I had. The girls made it extra special for me so I didn't feel the loss of you so much. Still very poignant though, Harry, to have to celebrate my birthday without you. I couldn't help but feel sad.

The girls had arranged for John and Eric to bring the children over for tea as well, so that I didn't have to come home to an empty house alone, on my birthday. We had our usual indoor picnic, and we set a plate for you on your chair, Harry.

While we were out after lunch we went to look at some furniture I had seen and liked.

Very modern, to go in my bungalow. After all, I was having everything new. From top to bottom. I chose some bedding which will dictate the colour scheme of my bedroom and I even found some curtains that blended very nicely with it. I had the window measurements with me and so set about having them made up to size. None of the 'that will do' this time Harry.

I am having it perfect first time. No more making do. No more buying rubbish with the view to replacing it with quality when we could afford it. None of it ever did get replaced, did it Harry? We looked after it so well that even cheap, crap furniture stood the test of time. Just *your* desk Harry. That was quality.

We would have quality Paula, I had plans for the house, Oh yes you have found them. When I retired I was going to take you away for an extended sailing holiday and while we were gone I planned to have the builders in to renovate the whole house. Just the way I always wanted it. Antique furniture in every room and new flooring throughout. You could have come home to a beautiful new albeit old home. I take it you didn't like my plans much but it would all have been done and sorted when we came home.

Tuesday 5th October.

Today Harry I am going to give up another part of you. Your big plush comfortable executive car is going. I have been looking at sports cars I like and have found one that I am going to buy. Your car is not new by any means and they will take it in part exchange for the nearly-new Mazda sports car that I am getting. It is British racing green. It has what they call a retractable roof, which means I can just push a button and the whole thing folds up and puts itself in the boot.

I know that you are going to tell me that it is the wrong time of the year to be buying an open top car and I will not get much use out of it until next spring. But on the other hand Harry, it's much cheaper to buy when everyone is getting rid of theirs. You see, although I now have all this money you left me and I am rich, I still can't get past the skinflint in me. The new car is tiny compared to your big tank of a car Harry, and although I have enjoyed driving that one. I think I will enjoy the sports car more. It's the new me. I am having all the fripperies on it. Build in sat nav, Bluetooth, Ipod dock, electric windows. I am so going to enjoy this Harry. I am really quite excited and it is even better than when I got my first car, which was Dad's choice.

This one is my choice. Today is the day, and then I will come home and take loads of pictures of it and send them to Jenny in Greece.

I will drive by the warehouse and show Eric and John. They have been very interested in my purchase and I'm sure they will have the bonnet up.

Then I have to go into the city to look in furniture shops. Although I know the colours in the new house I still have to decide on the actual furniture. Shall I have a nice comfortable corner sofa in the lounge or some of these chairs that recline with the push of a button? I need to make up my mind about that, something to do with power points set into the floor. The electrician took great pains to explain it all to me. I felt somewhat patronised by him as if he was waiting for my husband to make the decision that I would not understand.

I do find I have to fight my corner sometimes with these men and they expect my husband to 'Okay' my decisions.

Well, when you were here Harry I would have waited for you to make the final decision. I would have told them to wait till you got home or to ring you at the office. Knowing what I know now Harry, would you have been there? Or would you have been with Sharon?

No I mustn't start thinking about them now. I have stuff to do. A house to design. A home to make. One to feel comfortable in. And one to grow into and feel at one with my own company. I have just thought, Harry it is more than six months since you died.

I don't cry every day now. If I do cry it isn't so much for you or the fact that I am missing you but more that I am quite daunted by what I have to face. The rest of my life as one, not half of two. I also cry in frustration at what I have lost. Yes I have lost you but also I now know I have lost thirty two years to you. Years when you moulded me into a shadow of myself although a much bigger shadow, fatter shadow.

Was I too young to resist your all-powerful personality? Or did I just roll over and show my belly like a squirmy puppy? Was I so ready to fall into your life? I had plans. I was going to be a great artist, or at least do something arty with my life. I know it isn't too late, that I can still do it, but I feel that the choice was taken away from me. You even decided when it was time for me to get pregnant. You admitted that. You never wanted me to adulterate my body with chemicals like taking the pill, but you would be sure to use protection. Except of course when you decided it was time for me to have a baby.

Time for us to start a family, you said. But you didn't have to carry the child, did you Harry? Neither of my pregnancies was easy. I was ill most of the time and had to have almost weekly hospital appointments.

You made sure I got to them, taking me yourself. I was so grateful for the support. So solicitous, and kind. You looked after me and made sure I had the best of everything. I carried on working until nearly birth time with Molly as you said you would be able to be with me at a moment's notice if I needed anything. I thought that was the best as well, rather than be at home alone. I wanted to be with you. I nearly died giving birth to Molly. The doctor told us that we would be wise to consider leaving it at just the one child. You started using protection again. Molly thrived despite her difficult birth.

Then one night when we were getting passionate you 'forgot' your protection. Or did you tell me it split? I can't remember now but I got pregnant again with Sandi. I was worried that the same thing would happen again but I was better with her despite what the doctor had said. The hospital kept an even closer eye on me and towards the end I had to ring in every day to let them know how things were going. Sandi's birth was not too bad, I was unconscious for most of it, they made sure of that. But I can remember hearing the doctor having a right go at you for letting me get pregnant again.

Even with uneasy pregnancies and births you would always say we could have more. But you didn't know about the pill did you Harry? No, I was not going to go through that again. That was one secret I managed to keep from you. I don't need it now I am no longer fertile. Officially old. Now I just concentrate on the grandchildren.

I wanted a son Paula. Even if it meant losing you. But you failed in that as you did most things.

Wednesday 6ᵗʰ October

Paula went down to the pub and booked the whole family in for Christmas dinner.. She didn't feel that she wanted the first Christmas without Harry to be at home in the house. It would be very different. But then having an empty chair where Harry should be would have been even worse.

I also went to order our - my Christmas cards. You always said that it would make life easier for me if we had printed ones done so all I had to do was sign them and address the envelopes. How thoughtful of you Harry, I was grateful for your concern at the time.

Actually that was something we could have done together, instead you would just give me a list and expect the cards to be sent. I am not going to bother sending them to so many of our acquaintances this year, let's face it I haven't heard from them since the funeral so I am probably off their list anyway. I also had just my name put on them. You can hardly send Christmas greetings can you Harry?

The first Christmas without you, how will that go? I will have a tree up and the old decorations can come out. Then when it is all over they can all go in the bin. I will buy new ones for next year. Another way to cut the ties from you.

It's turned quite chilly now and Paula has put the heating up a bit more. After all she had a full tank of oil to use up.

I will not wander around this great big house in three jumpers and leggings under my dresses just to keep warm. As soon as you came home you turned the heat up so you could be comfortable but told me it was a waste to have it on in the day. After all with all the house work to be done I would hardly have time to get cold would I?

She also decided not to bother using the wood burner. That would just take a lot of cleaning. Paula didn't have time for that now. Just turn the knob if you want more heat, she thought to herself. Mrs. M. is very good but she has so much work to do already she really didn't want to put too much on her. Lugging all those logs indoors was always such a pain as well.

How this year is flying by Harry. Six whole months without you and I have achieved so much on my own.

Paula spoke with the estate agent regarding the price as there had been very few viewings. Perhaps they were asking too much for it? Would it be a good idea to actually put a modern kitchen in and keep the price up or not do that work and reduce the price? The agent said it may be an idea to get some new kitchen plans drawn up to show what could be done with it but probably not actually do the work.

So many things to think about Harry that I would never have the need to concern myself with when you were here. You dealt with all these things and I just carried on in my own little world.

Some days Paula found it really liberating to have to make her own choices but some days she found it very daunting.

Was it like that for you Harry?
    You always seemed so confident and seemed to know that each road you took was the correct one.
But some of your decisions were not always correct, were they? The road you took to becoming a heavy drinker, for instance. That road ended in your death. If you had not been drunk that night things would have been so much different. You wouldn't have sat down by that tree, for a start.

She was in a bit of a quandary, she didn't want to have the house left empty when she moved to her bungalow as it would deteriorate when left and the girls may not get a decent price for it. Then again she didn't want to be moving out until the bungalow is ready for me to move into.

They tell me that by the end of February everything should have been done and I can then get the carpets and flooring laid. That's still four months away, but that is not their fault. The poor builders have had to change so many things because I have changed my mind so often. Then I can have all the furniture delivered, put my new china and crockery in the kitchen make my bed and put my clothes in the wardrobe. Turnkey, as they call it in America. Walk in and start living.

That reminds me, when I pick up the Christmas cards I will need to order some change of address cards. I will have a new phone number as well for the land line. I will have to put this all in my diary. I never needed a diary before Harry. You would always remind me of things I had to do. You were my walking diary. I do miss that.

Thursday 7th October

Today I arranged transport for my horse to be delivered to the stable yard. I am getting really excited. He is coming on Saturday 16th and a really nice gentleman is going to pick him up and bring him in his horse lorry. I have the saddler booked for the following Monday.

The girls at the yard have told me about a huge shop where I can buy all the other things I will need for him and some new riding clothes for me. When they go out on the road now all the girls wear high-visibility jackets. I will get myself one of those, as well as some new boots, a new hard hat, and a camera so I can video us riding. Not essential, but sounds like fun. Molly and Sandi are coming with me to look in this shop and we will go in Molly's estate car. That way I can fit in all the stuff I intend to buy. Okay have a laugh if you like, I could probably have fitted it all in your car but that has gone now and I have my little sports car. Not practical, I hear you say. No, Harry, not at all practical but so much more fun.

I saw Sharon when I was in town. She has changed. She is no longer blonde but has a more natural colour, quite dark. Was it you who asked her to go blond Harry? Were you making her into a younger version of me? In a way I feel quite flattered if that is the case. But if you wanted me when I was slim, blonde and fashionable, why did you turn me into a frump? I will never understand your thinking. After all these years I still find I really didn't know the real Harry. That is so sad, when you think about it. Such a waste of all that time.

Seeing her took all the excitement of the new car, the horse, and the bungalow away from me and left me depressed and tearful again. I just wanted to come home to you. But you are not here and this house no longer feels like home. And so I cry.

Why are you crying, Sharon was none of your busines Paula, you didn't have to involve yourself in that at all. You keep saying that you are getting on so well and you can manage without me so why are you crying. You know I hate to see you cry. Not that it upsets me to see you sad. No my dear it's that you look so bloody ugly when you cry.

Friday 8th October

I didn't sleep well last night Harry. When I did fall asleep I had vivid dreams of you, of when we were young and you were so loving and caring. My every wish was granted, within limits as we couldn't afford expensive wishes. The romance we shared, and how you would leave me little notes telling me how much you loved me. How soon did those notes turn into reminders of something I had to do? How soon did they become lists of things you wanted done? In my dreams they happened quite quickly but in reality I know it took years for the love notes to become demands, orders.

Paula had been into shops looking at kitchen designs just in case she needed to install a new kitchen in order to get a good price for the house. One had insisted that they needed to come round to measure it up although she had explained to them that she would be unlikely to buy one.

She thought of the fantastic kitchen she could have had and the baking she would have been able to get into. But the kitchen had never inspired her and Harry was the cake maker in the family. So even if she didn't install it she could leave the design for the new owners so they could see one way of doing it at least. They would probably have their own ideas anyway.

They will be coming sometime this morning so I can go out this afternoon. I am going riding today on Nicholas.

We are getting to know each other quite well now, but I know you are not interested in all this Harry, but that is just what I need today to cheer me up. Then I am going to Sandi's for tea. So I have a busy day ahead. I do like to have plenty to do.

Enjoy it while you can my dear. It will all come to a sticky end you know. I don't know how many times I have to tell you that but you will   keep on struggling. And will have to sort yourself out as I won't be there. But I arranged it so you had plenty to do.

Although I have been surprised at how well you are doing you just don't have it in you. No you are not capable.

Saturday 9th October.

The children came back with me last night and we were late to bed. Well, late for Dee and Zoe anyway. They are such fun to be with. Of course I had to bring them home in Sandi's car. She will be round later to drop my car off and pick up the little darlings to take home. See Harry? It all works out even if I don't have a practical car, and, Sandi is pleased to drive mine once in a while. When I move into the bungalow I won't need a car to pick them up, we will be able to walk. We will be so much closer and I can see more of them.

Saturday 16th October

What a busy week it has been. All my days have been spent at the stables getting everything ready for Nicholas to arrive. His stable has a nice bed in it, his paddock is ready for him to come into and today he is coming. I will just spend the day with him, grooming, fussing him, and sitting with him.

I don't want him to get lonely and miss his friends. I expect the girls and their children are going to get bored with me talking about him, but I am so excited. There is only one fly in the ointment. The girl at the stable yard, who is friends with Sharon. She is being just a bit too friendly, and I can't help feeling that she has is some kind of agenda.

I don't trust her one bit. I really think she is trying to find a way to claim something from me for her friend's son, your son. It was *her* friend stealing *my* husband not me stealing hers. Well I expect she will tell me at some point. I am not going to let her spoil my fun.

Tuesday 19th October.

'What time will you be ready Mum, to go to this shop of yours?' Sandi asked Paula on the phone.

'Well I will go turn Nicholas out and muck out, pop home and have a shower and I can be ready for about 9 o'clock?

'Good, I am picking Molly up at nine so we will come straight on to you. See you soon.'

Yes, it's my big day out. I am going to buy that horse so much stuff. This is going to be fun. I know what size rugs he needs and I will have his old bridle with me so I can get a nice new one to fit him. Oh all sorts of stuff you would know nothing about Harry.

'Gosh, you have spent loads of money on this horse of yours, Mum,' Molly said as we were coming out of the shop.

'I could have spent a lot more but didn't think I would fit it in the car.' I answered her. 'And that is nothing compared to the cost of the saddle, not to mention the livery costs and all the rest of his expenses.' I looked at her shocked face and reminded her, 'my money, my hobby.'

Sandi piped up. 'Stop being like Dad, Molly. Mum can do what she likes with her money. I'm sure there will be plenty left when she has finished with it.'

'Oi. I'm not going yet.'

'I didn't mean anything by it, just observing.' Molly said grumpily.

'I noticed that there is a really nice pub just down the road; I think it is lunch time. We will be back in time for the kids to come out of school if we eat now.'

When we had ordered our lunch we sat down and Molly said, 'So what is it with this girl at the stables then Mum, the one who knows Sharon?'

'I was thinking about her yesterday, I just don't know about her. She is being rather too friendly, unnaturally so. It's not even as if we are of an age I just think she is up to something and Sharon is putting her up to it.'

'Can't be that, Sharon is getting married. Jake told Rachel at school that he has a new Daddy and they are moving away. Maybe she wants to tell you and doesn't know how?'

I am shocked Harry. I am stunned.

Paula' mouth dropped open but she quickly shut it again. She thought that the girls had not noticed as they were busy eating their lunch. Paula on the other hand didn't eat any of hers, she just pushed it around her plate.

She didn't know how to feel about this revelation. Shocked, stunned. She could feel the old hysteria bubbling up in her. She had to get out of there and be alone to digest this news.

126

'Mum, are you alright?' Both the girls looked worried. She shook herself out of her reverie and smiled at them.

'Well that's a turn up for the books.' She was in so much of a shock she got up and went to pay their bill, and downed a quick brandy while she stood at the bar.

'Think I had better be getting back.'

'Home it is then' Molly said.

'Not home, it doesn't feel like home any more. I don't know where home is but that house isn't home to me, not now.'

We drove via the stables so that I could drop everything off. No-one was there so I didn't have to face anyone. I went to give Nicholas a hug. I put his new rug on him as it is due to get cold tonight and he is going to stay out in his paddock. I gave him a fresh hay net and his tea so I need not come back later when the yard is full of people. I had some thinking to do before I faced the people there. I had to be alone to ponder this news.

Once I was back at the house again and the girls had left me I sat in the kitchen and started to shake. I could feel the hysteria rising in me. I knew I wasn't having a heart attack I knew it was a panic attack. I had to get this frustration out of me. I filled the kettle and set it to boil; thinking a cup of tea may help. I went to the dresser to get a cup but then I swept my hand along the shelf and knocked all the plates, cups and other things on the floor.

They crashed in a very satisfying way. I then eased myself round the side of the dresser and pulled with all my might and tipped it over. Such a noise it made as it hit the floor. Then the table was next, that went up and over as well. To my delight it broke, shattered. In the pantry all your cake tins came out one by one. Then the shelves in there were cleared with one sweep. After a while the hysteria began to calm down a bit and I sat in the middle of all this mess and cried. And cried, and cried some more. I was screaming, and crying shaking and sweating.

HARRY YOU ABSOLUTE BASTARD. YOU SHITTING, FUCKING EVIL BASTARD I yelled to no-one. I cried and cried and cried myself to sleep there, in the middle of all this mess.

'What about that then?' Sandi asked Molly as they were driving way after dropping their Mum off at the house.

'Dad must have had a fairly long term affair with this Sharon woman, but it didn't take her long to find another man did it?'

'Well I wonder if he wasn't always in the back ground. Is Jake really Dad's child? Or was she playing him off as well?'

'Bit suspicious isn't it'?

'Poor Mum was really taken aback about it wasn't she?'

'Yeah, I feel quite bad leaving her there alone.'
She went really white and didn't actually eat her lunch, did you notice?'

'Yes, I think I had better ask Eric to pop in on his way home and make sure she is alright.'

'Oh my God.'
It was Eric. Poor Eric, what a scene to walk into. He found a not-too-dented saucepan and boiled some water

to make tea. While he was doing this he was on the phone.

'Molly, better get round here, It's your Mum…No she isn't too happy. Better ring and see if John can come round and help as well. Yeah it's a bit of a mess in here.'

Next thing I knew I was sitting in the lounge with a cup of very sweet tea. Eric and John were trying to make sense of the kitchen. Eric must have found the only unbroken cup. Molly came as well and gathered some clothes for me and then we went to her house. Sandi met us there and they put me to bed in Molly's spare room. I slept. I was exhausted.

Wednesday 20th October.

When I woke up it was with that unfamiliar feeling Harry. You know the one, where for a few seconds you don't know who you are, where you are and what you have been doing? Then the realisation came to me that I had trashed the kitchen. Well it's a good job I didn't trash the rest of the house.

'Cup of coffee Mum? Just how you like it; with plenty of whole milk.'

'Thanks darling, that's kind of you. I should get up. What time is it'?

'Half nine. The kids have gone to school and we can spend the morning sorting out the rest of the kitchen. Eric and John dumped everything last night. Nothing was worth keeping. But it was crap anyway. Oh Mum, if you felt like that why didn't you stay here or ask one of us to stay with you?'

Paula smiled sadly at Molly and said, 'I didn't know how I felt until I got home. I just went into a blind panic. I really didn't know what I was doing but I was so angry.'

'You should stay here until your bungalow is ready?'

'Nice thought darling, but I have to go back and face things. I am feeling much better, it's just that I am finding out so much that I never knew about your father. It's going to be ages before the bungalow is ready, and I have to be there to sell the house anyway, I can't leave it empty. It will seem cold and lifeless, so I had better go back and see what I need to replace.

'Well, I'll make you some breakfast before we go, we will need to swing by the supermarket on the way. Eric and John brought that old table in from the barn for the kitchen and all the chairs were alright. But you'll need a few saucepans, a kettle, some stock pantry foodie bits, just enough to keep you going till you move. You get dressed and I'll see you downstairs when you're ready.'

'God, I expect there will be some cleaning to do.'

'Nope, Sandi and I cleaned it all up, and John has found some paint in the barn to do the wall where the dresser stood. Don't think that had been moved in a while had it?'

It looked very different, Harry, when I walked in lugging bags of shopping. New saucepans, new kettle, a plastic table cloth to cover up that cranky old table. Some new crockery, a small cheap set that can live in the pantry. I told Molly I didn't need stock items like flour, you did all the cake making and baking. I hadn't tipped over the fridge so I still had some food. So with a lot of help from the girls, we made it look presentable. I like it much better without that nasty old dresser.

Paula didn't use the magnolia paint that John found in the barn. She popped out to the hardware store and bought some blackboard paint. Yes you can still get it. It is basically black matt emulsion paint. When everyone had gone again she painted a big circle of black on the wall where the dresser had stood.

It is nearly a circle Harry, it's the best I can do on these uneven walls.

Stupid bitch, how dare you take your anger out on my House? What a mess you made and then conveniently fell asleep so someone else had to clean it up. Typical! And what the hell is that on my wall.

Monday 25th October

Its half term and I am having the children over today. They will see the blackboard wall for the first time Harry. I am sorry you are missing this. You would have enjoyed having them over. It is one of the weeks you always took off work, so you could be with them. You always said it was the best of the school holidays because for all the other children were with their parents and this one we could have with them, just not all at once.

You were right, by now the parents were exhausted and needed a rest. So today is the start of the Granny week. Just me this time, but as we proved in the summer we can do this, the kids and me. We won't have the garden to play in as it is raining, but we have the black wall and I have devised lots of games to involve it.

'WOW, Grandma! A black wall. Cool,' Daniel gushed as they came in.

'Here you go, there are the chalks. Get creative.'

Robotic monsters, from Daniel, flowers from Rachel.

The twins' scribbles are supposed to represent fairies. If you squint you can just see them. But the thing is, they all had fun.

The wall kept the kids occupied all morning. I hadn't even started on the games I had devised for them.

They didn't seem to notice that you weren't here Harry. Do they just accept that you are gone? Am I nasty to think that they are having more fun with me than if you had been here? Sad to say, I am beginning to think so. Thing is Harry, we do more.

When you were here they would be watching television and you would be reading or cooking them a fancy cake, or taking them out to fancy restaurants for lunch. Did you think that was a treat for them? They're children, they want to play.

Alright, I do admit that sometimes Daniel would rather be playing on his Xbox or something but I can say Harry, that he joined in all the games so nicely, I was so proud of him. I have so much love for these children. It's just a shame that you are missing all this love. They used to really enjoy cuddling you and sitting with you while you watched their programmes. Or did you fall asleep with them all sitting on you while they watched?

Still they loved being with you, and the cuddles. But you are not here to give the cuddles. I love the cuddles, just before bedtime.

And often during the day. I get cuddles from all of them, even Daniel who considers himself too big and grown up to cuddle his grandma out in public.

They are staying over tonight, then home after tea tomorrow for the rest of the week because the girls think I will be too tired if I have to cater for their children all week. Probably right, after my flip out last week. And I have to admit I do get tired, especially when I am on my own. Thinking about it I am lucky that the girls allowed me to look after their children at all after last week. So lucky. I was also lucky that the morning after my kitchen trashing episode John had gone up to the stables and fed Nicholas his breakfast. He reported in that the horse was fine and as it was to be a warm day he had even taken Nicholas' rug off.

Even got the family running about sorting your horse for you. So much for wanting a horse you are dumping the poor animal on everyone else.

Friday 5th November
The children had been with Paula most the previous week during the day. They had been dropped off or she had picked them up after seeing to Nicholas. Now she was feeling a bit lonely again because all half term week the house was full of noise and fun. There were a few tears when little the girls got tired but all in all a very good week.

This week I have been riding really early every day as the weather has been really lovely. Nicholas is proving to be such good company. I am so glad I got him. I know Harry. You would not approve but I have him now and he fills my days. Daniel had a ride on him last week and really enjoyed it, he said. he wants to come again. If he takes to it I shall buy a pony for the children to ride.

Today is, of course bonfire night, and we are having a firework party in the garden. I was always your job to light the fireworks and set the fire going.

Well we'll have a really big fire this year, consisting of the old kitchen furniture, that horrible dresser and table. I always said that nothing was forever. Well, that dresser will find its own forever and burn. That envelope of photos that you had taped behind the top drawer. I presume they are of Jake. Or were there others? Other children that I knew nothing of? Well, they will burn too. That part of your life I will forget. I am drawing a line under your extra marital activities. You were still my husband when you died and that makes me your widow.

Molly and Eric are coming over after work with John, but Sandi is bringing the children straight from school. Things are going to get messy in the kitchen because they want to prepare the after fire tea party. I have left it to them exactly what we have to eat.

The evening went well. John and Eric lit the fire and the fireworks were marvellous, with all the Ooohs and Aaahs coming from the children. No accidents no dud fireworks that needed re-visiting. It was very cold outside and the children had little red noses but it was nice and warm indoors. We were just about settling down to our indoor picnic of baked potatoes with beans followed by jelly that had not quite set and which we had to pour over ice-cream.

Then it happened. Eric felt unwell. He went very white and said he felt faint. I called the doctors emergency number but could not get through. Then the hospital to ask what to do and they said call 111. They in turn told me to call an ambulance.

Sandi rang 999. Eric by this time was saying he felt better but then collapsed on the kitchen floor. Daniel and Rachel were of course very upset and we tried to comfort them while we got Eric to the couch in the lounge. I went to get some extra blankets from our bed. No duvet, you didn't like them did you Harry?

I called 999 again and they said an ambulance was on its way but had been diverted to a firework display where there had been a terrible accident. They said that as Eric was conscious we were not considered a priority but they would send one as soon as they could.

Molly was trying to make Eric comfortable; John and Sandi were keeping the children occupied. I went into melt down, I felt I should be able to sort this situation out but was at a loss. I didn't know what to do. Harry, you would have been able to take control here and I am sure you would. We all wondered if we should just take Eric to the hospital ourselves.

Molly, quite rightly said that we would be waiting around in A&E for him to be seen because it is always really busy on bonfire night. I wondered if that would upset the children even more if their father was taken away. So we decided to wait it out, but Eric didn't seem to be getting any better and we had no idea what, if anything to give him. Had he had a heart attack? There was, it seemed to be no help to hand.

Eric was not feeling any better but he could talk and said he didn't feel any more ill than he had felt earlier. He said he didn't hurt but was just so weak and felt nauseous. His head, he said, was spinning and thought a car journey would make him feel even worse.

At least he was conscious and able to tell us how he felt. I cast around in my mind anyone we knew who had medical experience but could not think of anyone. But he needed real medical attention. In the end I managed to gain some control and decided we would in fact take him to the hospital. I reasoned that even if we had to wait for a while at least he would be there and any medical attention he might need could be accessed straight away. So we went. Molly, Eric and myself.

Sandi and John stayed at home with the children. I had my mobile with me so we could tell them how we were getting on.

It was chaos at the hospital. There were children with burns, adults also with burns. Children with food poisoning from uncooked food, some who had become over excited and needed to be sedated. Ambulances turning up constantly, blue lights flashing.

Sandi had phoned through to 999 to tell them to stand down the call to us. And there we waited. Of all the nights for poor Eric to fall ill he had to choose what was probably the busiest one of the year. By about half past ten things were beginnings to calm down a little bit. It was raining really hard by now and most of the displays and private celebrations were coming to an end.

Eventually he was admitted. They didn't know what was wrong with him either and were doing a lot of tests. It was with sadness and concern that we had to leave him there and go back to the house. Molly wanted to stay but the kindly nurse said it would be better if she could go home and get some rest. Well, that was unlikely, but at least she could be there for her children while we all waited to see what had happened to Eric.

All this indecision Harry. I know you would have taken control and done the right thing. But you were not here to take control, were you Harry? When I needed you, Molly needed you, Daniel and Rachel needed you. Sandi and John had coped admirably with the children. She had put hers to bed and was playing a card game with Daniel and Rachel when we arrived home at about 1.30 am. John was upstairs with Zoe and Dee. We sat in the kitchen and drank endless cups of tea. Molly tried to rest but decided to go back to the hospital at four in the morning. Eric was still asleep and sweating. She rang us to let us know how he was and we could only sit and wait.

Harry, what would you have done now? Probably, you would have got on with some jobs to keep busy. You would not have shown any emotion but would get on with life. People used to think you were hard and uncaring. But I knew better Harry. I knew that was how you dealt with your worries. You filled your days with doing stuff. Any stuff but you had to keep busy. I, on the other hand, would sit and brood. I would start jobs but never finish them, flitting from one thing to another with the worry never far from my mind. I could never settle to anything. I couldn't this time. I just wanted to hear that Eric was going to be alright.

Eric stayed in hospital for nearly a week. We never did know what was wrong with him. Over work? A flash virus? Exhaustion? We never found out. But he came home and after a few more days resting he went back to work and so far has not had any further problems. What a relief. What an awful time it was.

Poor Molly was very worried and upset. I know she would have gone to you for comfort Harry. She always was a Daddy's girl. But she only had me and I felt that I came up short.

Yes but don't you always my dear. You have never really come up to my expectations. You married me under false pretences and that happy, confident, intelligent, and ambitious girl I thought I loved? Somehow I got you.

Monday 15th November.

Well, that weekend was a bit hectic but things have calmed down now with Eric home and feeling fine.
The weather has improved so I am going riding with some of the other girls from the yard. We are going to load the horses up in lorries and take them to the beach. I don't think Nicholas has ever been to the beach so this may be rather more exciting than normal.

I am going with Sharon's friend, so I expect to be hearing all about the upcoming wedding. Apparently Trish is going to be the maid of honour. I still don't really trust her but so far she has been nothing but friendly and she seems to have decided that I will be her riding buddy. Perhaps she just feels sorry for me.

She has never mentioned you again so maybe I am just being overly suspicious and she really didn't connect me with Sharon's partner. Now Harry, I find that I can listen to all the wedding talk in a very detached manner.

I think I am past caring about you and your affair. That's if there was only one. Those photos, that went on the bonfire? Who were they I wonder. But I think I really cannot be bothered with any of it any more. Live my life without you and just get on. I will be out all morning and then will come back, tidy myself up and then go to see how the building work is coming on.

Those boys are doing a lovely job on my bungalow Harry. I am really looking forward to living there.

There had only been a few viewings on the house and even those had dried up now.

Paula discussed it with the estate agent and they decided to leave the price as it was for now but perhaps bring it down a bit after Christmas.

'You really don't want people traipsing around at this time of year anyway do you? The agent asked Paula.

'So you think it will be more of a spring sale then?' She asked.

'I think you're right it's probably best to forget this year and look to next year and give it a push', the agent advised.

Whoever buys it will have so much work to do. The, stuff we put up with because we had lived here so long. Ill-fitting draughty windows; doors that don't really hang straight, loose handles and catches. The whole place needs a good decorating and I really can't be bothered to get it done. Your desk is at Molly's house and there is no other furniture I want to take with me, there is nothing here of any value or even quality so when the house does sell I will get house clearance people in to clear it out fully.

I have been to choose my carpet, yes, one shade of carpet for the whole of the bungalow and the colours of the walls will blend throughout the house. It has been so much fun deciding on my colour scheme. I have bought all the furniture, or ordered it anyway.

Some of it will be ready to go in as soon as the carpets are fitted, some I have to wait for. I have designed the kitchen just how I want it, with a breakfast area. The two bathrooms are now finished and looking really nice. Tomorrow, I am going into the city to find curtains for the lounge and two other bedrooms, I already have the ones for the master bedroom or should that be the mistress bedroom as it is mine?

I may have to have them made up so I have a pad with all the window sizes which I will take with me along with the colour swatches and a piece of the carpet. It is going to be really superb. Probably not to your taste Harry. In fact I know you will not like it. That's fine, it will be my taste. Now that I am beginning to know just what my taste is.

Certainly not to my taste. I am surprised that you would fall for the fashion thing Paula. I thought I had instilled at least a bit of taste in you in all the years I had been trying. But you are going against me and everything I wanted of you.

Tuesday 16th November.

It was glorious on the beach with the horses yesterday. Nicholas would not go anywhere near the sea, but so long as another horse was between him and the waves he was alright. Funny boy! I do love him and am so enjoying getting back to my first love as a hobby. It gives me something to get up and out for as I have to go and see him twice a day. It was a bit hectic when the children were here, getting them all out, reminded me of the days when the girls were young and getting them ready for school in the morning.

But the children had fun at the stable yard and Daniel was such a help. I really think he will want to take it up. I will have to think about getting a pony for him. I may discuss that with Molly when I see her later. She is coming with me today to the city to carry stuff and I don't doubt give me her considered opinion of the curtain colours I should have. Well, if I like her choice I may listen to her but I don't have to I can choose for myself.

'Daniel enjoyed his week with you Mum. He has started talking of wanting a pony,' Molly said before Paula could even broach the subject. They had just sat down to have a spot of lunch in a big store cafe.

'Shall I organise some lessons for him?' She asked. 'He really needs to be able to ride first.'

'Yes, that's what I told him. There is a riding school attached to the livery yard, isn't there?'

'Yes, he can come on Saturday mornings and have some lessons and then come on the yard and learn how

141

to look after a pony.   'How about Rachel, is she interested?'

'I think she will be if Daniel is.'

'How about you?'

'Never really got into it as kids, did we, Sandi and me? It was something I thought about but then Dad took us sailing and I sort of forgot about riding.'

'But you enjoyed your sailing didn't you?'

'Oh yes, we both loved it. And it took up all our spare time so we didn't think about riding then.'

'So, why don't you all come along? Sandi as well if she wants to.'

'Well, we could have a few lessons and just see how we get on and if we like it. I know I would like to give it a try.'

'Oh by the way are you all coming to dinner on Sunday? Sandi and family are so I thought we would see if we can get one uneventful family dinner in.'

'Sounds good, what are you planning, A roast?'

'Yeah, I have an enormous joint of pork in the freezer, it needs eating. If you're all coming I'll get it out to defrost. Now let's go look at some more curtains.'

It feels good, Harry to have at least some of the family interested in my hobby. I feel vindicated after all this time, and valued, as if it is at least as important as your pastimes. This is something I have never felt before. It had always been brushed aside to make way for the sailing and shooting. I carried on with my shopping with a new light step and a happy heart.

Friday 19th November

All the family had arrived for the roast pork dinner which Paula had managed to cook with no disasters. She had even cleared the dining room of clutter from the attic so they could all fit round the big table in there. They got out all the crockery, none of which matched since she had broken most of it, but they managed and had a lovely happy family meal. They talked about her new bungalow and she decided that it was time that Molly and Sandi came to see the progress. So they arranged a time and day for them to come and have a look.

We also talked about the riding lessons and it was decided that I would arrange some lessons for Molly, Daniel, Rachel, Sandi and John, who had also expressed an interest. I know a nice lady who has a Shetland pony she said Dee and Zoe could have a sit on as well. I am really beginning to look forward to this, Harry. Eric is feeling fine now although I don't suppose we will ever find out what made him so ill that day. It is just a relief to know he is alright.

I do notice that Molly is taking more care of him. Not that I thought she neglected him but she gives him more attention. She seems to appreciate him a bit more, perhaps she has realised she also would be lost without him as I still, sometimes feel lost without you. The children are very excited about the riding lessons. Daniel, of course, told the younger girls that he had already ridden Nicholas and he thought he would be really good at it.

I had a quiet smile to myself about his bragging, and caught Molly with a smirk on her face as well. We flashed the raised eyebrows 'he'll learn', look at each other. So next Saturday will be the big day for the lessons. I have already spoken with the yard owner and provisionally booked a group beginners lesson.

She knows what to expect and has an idea of the age range. I just have to add John into the mix. We couldn't persuade Eric to have a go. He said he was nervous around horses but would happily look after the little ones while the lesson was happening. He said he would supervise the Shetland sit-on with Zoe and Dee.

It was a happy meal and for once we found we didn't spend the whole time thinking that Harry should be there.

That empty chair Harry. It wasn't empty. We didn't keep a portion of food for you, as if you were just late home. This is the first time that we have had meal and you were not the focus of all our thoughts. What does this mean Harry? Are we beginning to get used to you not being here? I loved the day but it did feel strange that we could all enjoy our company without a feeling of loss. We didn't miss you Harry.

Really, if that is so why are you so busy pointing out to me how much you didn't miss me?

Saturday 20th November

So Harry! The big day, for the riding lessons. Daniel phoned me last night. He was so excited. Rachel was a bit nervous, he said but he would look after her.

I am going to the yard at 7 o'clock this morning to do the stable for Nicholas and ride him and then the rest of them are coming at 11 o'clock for the lesson. Susan, the instructor, will need a hand to get the ponies ready.

So I really need to be finished by ten thirty so I can help with the tacking up. She asked me for sizes. John is six feet tall so he will need something quite large.

Molly and Sandi are both about five feet six inches and Daniel at the tender age of eleven is as tall as me. Which at only five feet is nothing to brag about. Rachel is still quite small at about four feet tall. So Susan knows which ponies and horses she will use.

There are always helpful children at a riding stable who are ready and willing to hold horses, tack them up and run with them. It is a rite of passage for most young children who want to ride. They do the work for free at the weekends and get to ride for their payment.
It's an age old custom and is also how I started to learn stable management.

So the lesson began. Paula stood on the side lines of the school and was interested to see who took to it and who really didn't want to do it. Sandi did really well she was a natural. She found her seat and control within minutes. Molly took a little longer, Daniel loved it and will be a good rider. Rachel just wanted to hug the pony.

John, on the other hand, will take a few lessons before he gets the hang of it. He was bouncing around on that poor horse but expressed his delight. He said he loved it and will work hard to get the seat he needs to sit properly.

Eric was enjoying himself with Paula's friend Anne, who was popping Dee and Zoe on the Shetland pony and giving them small rides up and down the yard. They did have fun but Paula was not sure they would bother again. Dancing is more their thing.

'So who wants to come next week and do it all again then?' Susan asked. Rachel said she was not really interested and would rather play with the Shetland pony. Daniel, jumped up and down yelling, 'me me me!'

Sandi and Molly both said they would love to. John asked if he could have a private lesson.

'So next week we have three for group lesson and a private one for John. Is that right?' Susan asked.

'Well I could come during the week one evening if that is possible'' John said.

'Of course you can. We have the indoor school we use in the evenings and on rainy days,' Susan assured him.

All booked for next week. Now it seemed that they would have to make a visit to the tack shop to buy hard hats, body protectors and all the other riding gear needed.

Oh Harry, I am in my element. I love this. My children want to do something I really love and share it with me. After all these years of me feeling side-lined, of tagging along. They can actually appreciate something I have always loved. Something that is mine, not yours, Harry.

You and your bloody horses they will be the death of you, mark my words. Paula you know I don't like you doing that and now you are forcing it on our children. I am not happy about any of this my woman. Not at all.

Tuesday 23rd November.
The builders have finished at the bungalow. I have hired a team of people to clean it up ready for the decorator to

come in. I certainly do not intend to do any of this work. There is still a skip in the driveway and when the clearing up is done I can have that taken away. I have been spending all my spare time making pattern boards with the curtain materials and carpet sample so I know what colours to have on the walls.

When I look at home decorating magazines they all seem to have this accent wall. That's a dark wall or one with garish wall paper, but I am not sure I like that. I prefer to have pictures up to give accent.

I have been looking through the old photos and have taken some to be enlarged and put on canvas.

I think I will have a family wall. You will be there Harry, but you are only going to be a small picture. I will make this wall mainly of living people. You will be in a small group with your parents and mine. I don't want you overshadowing me again.

I am really beginning to feel free of you. I suppose it is only a few months since you died and maybe I have not grieved enough or not at all. I'm sure a psychologist would tell me I am nasty, selfish, or have a narcissistic personality disorder, but I have found out so much about you and I have to admit I don't actually like most of it. I still wonder how I let you control me the way you did. It was very subtle, so much so that it was only after you had died that I realised that you had been controlling me.

Molly and Sandi are beginning to see just how much of my life was wrapped up in yours. How mine faded into the background while you shone like a bright star. Well, it is my turn to shine. It wasn't all bad though. I did love you even if I was not in love with you. We had some great times together and we enjoyed each other's company.

I felt safe with you and comfortable and I knew you loved me in your way. We were like an old pair of slippers, a bit saggy and worn but comfortable. I must not start looking back on our marriage and regret any of it because we were good together and we fitted. But I think still that was because I fitted to you and had to fit myself into your shape. You didn't bend to me at all.

But I digress, I was telling you about my pattern boards. I will be meeting the decorator at the bungalow later. Once it has been cleared, he will be able to tell me how much it will all cost and how long it will take him to do. I have already told him that I am not in any rush but also it must not take forever.

I have to admit that they do confuse me, some of these tradesmen. They talk about doing it at 'day rate', which I take to mean they charge a certain rate for each day. However many days it takes.

I have not fallen for that one yet, I have always asked for best estimates of cost and time. Which may in fact cost me more. It's not that we haven't got the money, or should I say I haven't got the money, but I just like to know how much it all is going to be. I did ask the builders to put up rails so then I can have the curtain person round once the carpets are in to measure. No more big gaps or loads of material hanging around getting in the way. My curtains will fit my windows.

So, it is all coming together and I am getting really excited about it all Harry. Even if it is still a good few months yet before I can move in, planning it is fun.

Have your fun, enjoy it while you can but I very much doubt if you will like living there. You have been shaped to fit my lifestyle, I made sure of that. But we will see.

Thursday 25th November

I have written and posted all the Christmas cards Harry. Just signed 'with love Paula.' Wow that was really quite hard. I sat myself down at the big table and went through the address book. I sent cards to everyone in the end even though I had already said that I would only send them to whoever I had heard from since your funeral. I will use the standard of seeing who I get one back from, and they will be the people who get the change of address cards.

The estate agent phoned me earlier today to say that she has someone who wants to come and view this house. They want to come tomorrow afternoon. Good job Mrs. M. is in tomorrow morning. She can give the place a real going over and I will get the lounge cleared of the last of the clutter. I have been systematically clearing all your old stuff and all those frocks of mine. There isn't much left now because quite a lot of it went on the bonfire. I have sorted all your presentable clothes and taken them to the charity shop so there are only a few things I need to sort out. The old house is looking as good as it can under the circumstances. They are coming with the agent at 2 o'clock. I will make myself scarce, I think. I'm not sure I can deal with this.

Mrs. M. has been doing a grand job of cleaning, tidying and general de-cluttering. She keeps the old house tidy and as clean as I need and like it to be. I have never been one to have the place spotless, after all my old gran always used to say that we had to eat a peck of dirt before we die. It was you, Harry that needed it to be bacteria free. Mrs. M. lives in town and will come to be my cleaner in the bungalow.

I don't want to lose her, she is one in a million.

I can feel you getting angry with me Harry. I know you don't want this. I can also feel you are unhappy that I am taking control. That I am making decisions. That I am walking away from our home. Even from your grave, you can make me feel guilty. I feel your wrath so much that I nearly cancelled the appointment. But I am a big girl now, I can call the shots.

Call the shots? You wouldn't know how to call any shots you are just a stupid woman and I hope you don't think that you look attractive without all that blubber you use to carry around. You now look scraggy and no one will be attracted to that I can assure you.

Friday 26th November

Oh my goodness, they like it. The family that viewed yesterday want to buy the house. They offered £20,000 less than the asking price but as the agent and I were discussing lowering the price I feel that is acceptable. They do have a place to sell before they can go ahead. They said they would need that £20,000 to make alterations, like a new kitchen, and bathrooms and new windows. I secretly thought that they would need much more than that. I hope they are not going to do what we did a quick cheap spruce up and then just leave it. But then again it isn't my problem.

Molly thought that Paula had done well, considering the state of the place. She said that she wouldn't have paid that much for it as it stands. Praise indeed. She and Sandi are pleased with the price and at least they have an idea of their inheritance value.

Now that it comes to it Harry. I don't know how I feel. Why am I sad? It's what I want. Or have I just been rebelling all this time? Would I have been happy to stay here? I feel my resolve wavering. Somehow my confidence that was so hard to get back is fading. I'm not so sure that this is what I want. Oh Harry. I need you to tell me I am doing the right thing. I need your blessing here. I'm falling into a pit of despondency and I can't seem to claw my way out. I doubt myself now. My life was so full of promise and ideas but I'm not sure that I want to go now. I just want to huddle indoors under a blanket and never come out.

That can't happen. I have commitments now. I have to get out in the mornings to go to Nicholas and see to his needs. That at least gets me up and out. It's raining so I shall not be riding today. I'll come straight home when he is sorted and perhaps do some cooking or something.

Ahh! You've found out that you really can't do without good old Harry have you? Trying to rebel against all I have taught you Paula? I knew you would fail and come to your senses. You need me to guide you and control your life. You can't do it alone, you know very well you can't. I have told you what you should do for so long that you are now floundering around like a beached whale. Just who do you really think you are? Paula, you are no-one without me.

Mrs. M. found her sitting at the kitchen table with a cold cup of tea. She took one look and hugged her. She could see that the depression had hit. What is it Harry? Fear? Nerves? Anxiety? Or am I really doing the wrong thing for all the wrong reasons?

'You need to see your doctor. You need some bereavement counselling,' she told me.

'But it's been months,' I said.

'I know but you have been doing so much, filling your days, keeping busy. You haven't allowed yourself to grieve properly.'

She said that when she lost her husband she hit a low about six months after he had died.

'It's taken bit longer for you but it is part of the process.' She had seen a counsellor and had been told of the stages of grief. Mrs. M, still had the number for her counsellor who had been recommended by her doctor. She wrote it down for me. I may make an appointment.

Why has this just hit me now? Everything was coming together nicely. House bought, horse bought, house sold. So why am I having all these doubts? Can I really do this all by myself? Or did I think I could and really can't manage without you Harry? Who do I think I am? I am no-one. Just one half of a couple and the other half, the strong half, has gone. I can't do this, I can't make this decision all by myself. Harry, I need you here to do it for me.

Why am I still here, why am I still alive, what use am I? No use at all, I can't even live a life alone. I can't, I just want to crawl into a big black bed and go to sleep forever.

Mrs. M, was still sitting next to me and I realised I have said all this out loud. She was holding my hand and said soothing things to me. She asked if she should phone the counsellors and see if she can get me an appointment. I just nodded. But then asked her to just give me the phone number I will ring.

Monday 29th November.

I got up and went to see Nicholas, to put him out in his paddock and did the stable ready for him to come into at night. This is daily routine, but today it was done with no joy, it seemed like a chore. I didn't stop to chat but come straight home. I felt the need to be here. Why?

For the last few months since you died Harry, I have only wanted to get out of the place, but now it seems like the only place to be, my safe haven. What have I been doing all this time? Running around like a headless chicken trying to push you and anything directly connected with you out of my life. I sat in the kitchen, looking out towards the copse.

Wanting to go there, but why? I was unable to get myself moving even to walk that far. I just sit. Staring at the copse as if waiting for you to emerge. I feel so bereft but I can't cry. I just want to sit here and fade away. To go to sleep, and want to sleep for ever and never awaken. To hide under a big black blanket. I never want to leave this kitchen again, I just want to stay here and be with you. I am looking for you, feeling you here with me, calling me to be with you.

Is that where I should be, with you Harry? Perhaps then I can be happy again. Maybe the world would be a better place to be if left it and came to you.

At 4 o'clock, I dragged myself back to the stable yard and got Nicholas into his stable for the night, gave him his tea and a hay net. He is quiet, he knows something is wrong. He tried to stop me from leaving, nuzzling into me and demanding attention. But I needed to be home again, safe in my, our, kitchen.

To just to sit and watch the copse. Even though it is pitch black out there I watch into the darkness. It feels so right to be waiting for you to come in from there.

You could always come and join me Paula, you don't need to stay there. They girls are grown and don't need you. They will get on fine without your interference in their lives. I am actually missing you but it's the crying I can't stand. You are not abiding by Harry's law are you? But do I really want to spend eternity with you? I would have to start training you all over again. Perhaps I need to break the hold, let you go.

Tuesday 30th November

That's where Mrs. M. found Paula, just sitting in the kitchen It seemed that she had been sitting there all night and had only roused herself to go back to the stables to carry out the daily routine for Nicholas. When Paula got back and Mrs M had arrived there was even more of an emptiness about the place. Harry had faded. Her presence pushed him away, but Paula could hear him calling and she knew she had to go and find him.

Where are you Harry?

154

She walked down to the copse to see if she could find him.

I feel closer to you again there but not close enough. I need to be with you Harry. You are calling me, and I need to find you. Harry. Oh Harry. I know you want me to join you and I feel powerless to stay away from you. Your control over me is still so great that I know I have to do as you ask. I have to come to you. I do not belong in this world. I belong with you. I will sit by your tree and wait for you.

Mrs. M. came out to try to get Paula indoors but she said she was waiting for Harry that she must stay there and he would come to fetch her.

I knew I had to stay there, cold and wet as I was I needed to be where you were, I told her. She went back to the house and I could see she was worried.

I was in a dream like state sitting right there by the tree on the cold ground, right where you had been sitting that night. I have fallen into this dark place and you have been dragging me down into it. I have to struggle up again. I can't let this happen. I have so much to live for and can't take another parent away from the girls. They are still grieving for you I can't let them go through all that again. Sad as I feel right now I have to live and carry on without you. No Harry, I am not coming with you. However much you may call me I am staying right here. I am strong. I will fight you, and this terrible sadness.

Paula went about her daily business and settled into a pattern, but she still have this abiding feeling of terrible sadness, emptiness. She knew that Mrs, M and the girls were worried about her present mood, but she tried to put on a smile whenever they were near her. When alone she was enveloped in to the darkness again.

I have this black blanket draped over me all the time, I know I should be able to shake it off but it won't budge. I am doing everything I like to do. Riding, looking after Nicholas. Talking with friends, meeting people for coffee, Skyping people that don't live near. And so it goes on. But I am not enjoying any of it. That saddens me because I was coping really well and had thought I was through the worst. I have read all the leaflets again that Liz left me about bereavement and realise that I need some help here.

Tuesday 14th December

'Depression is a serious illness. You probably would benefit from some counselling, and I am going to prescribe some anti-depressants for you.' The doctor told her.

Paula just nodded. Feeling so weak and drained that she didn't have the energy to argue with him. It had taken all this time to pluck up the courage to go to the doctor. But having finally got there she felt relief that he was taking her feelings seriously.

'My family think I need some counselling.'

'I can give you a referral, to begin with and yes, that would be good for you. I don't like prescribing pills here there and everywhere but I think you need a bit of extra help. I can prescribe some antidepressants.

'We have to start you on a low dose and you might experience some side effects. They will take a while before you really begin to notice any difference but soon we can increase the dose.'

Harry would never have approved of her taking tablets, but Harry is not here and he is not going through all this.

So Paula left the surgery clutching a prescription and went directly to the pharmacy. One a day, was told she should take and they may make her feel sleepy, so best take them at night just before bed, the pharmacist told her.

When I went to Molly's she hugged me. I felt the love from her.

'You were doing so well, Mum.'

'I know, everything seemed to be going along nicely. Then I got the offer for the house and it all just crashed down around me. I suddenly wasn't so sure that was what I wanted. All of a sudden it became a reality and I got frightened. I have been waking up at ridiculous times of the night and not able to get back to sleep. I find myself sitting staring either out of the window or even in the mirror, just looking. I'll take the pills and find a counsellor to talk it through.'

'Good, you are going to need all the strength you have. Apparently moving house is one of the most stressful things you can do and it comes right on top of the loss of Dad. You can always stay there you know, there is no pressure on you to move out. We are here for you, you know that and we will help, especially with all the physical stuff. I did wonder if it was the right thing to do, and tried to tell you so.'

'Yes, I know you did but this would probably have happened anyway I'm told. 'Talking therapy', that's what they recommend, I can't carry on like this I feel so useless.'

So I've started taking the pills, Harry. I can feel your disapproval. You would have said that I could pull myself together if I wanted to but I just don't have the strength on my own. I don't expect miracles, I know it will take some time and that I have to get on with life. I realise now it had been building up for ages and I maybe should have expected something like this.

I thought had found a new strength and that I could be happy to live on my own. Maybe I still can Harry.

You are not here so I have to. It is hard and the black blanket is a comfort to me, but I know I need to try to live without that as well.

Every day I put on a happy face and try to hide the black blanket and it works because not many people notice that I am dying inside. Every night I go to bed and hope that I won't have to wake up in the morning.

Each morning when I wake I curse that I haven't just died in the night. I can't get proactive and actually kill myself, but I don't want to be in this world. Do I want to be with you Harry? I just don't know. Do I want to move out of this house? I don't know. I could just stay here and be close to you, forever. I make myself go out and see people, but all I really want to do is just sit here and wallow in my own misery, which in itself is strange because I still feel that the house doesn't like me or want me here.

The doctor says that in a couple of weeks I may start to notice a difference in my mood, because of the tablets he has given me. I can't see an end to this, though. I can't look that far ahead. I wonder how long I will have to wait to see a counsellor. I can afford to pay one and don't have to wait. Mrs. M gave me a phone number but I haven't rung yet. Why not? I just don't have the motivation.

It's cold and wet outside which suits my mood perfectly. I go to see Nicholas and sometimes in between showers I ride out with the girls. That goes some way to lift my mood. But I have to force myself to do it. I chat, I laugh and joke. Then I come home to this black-hearted oppression. But I can't leave, can't just walk away.

Paula made up her mind that she really needed help to bring her out of this depression. She made the phone call. On Monday after she had been to Nicholas she had arranged an appointment.

Meanwhile I have to prepare for Christmas. At least I don't have to get much food in for the meal, just afternoon tea. You haven't made a Christmas cake this year so I will have to buy one, and I will buy mince pies and sausage rolls as well, plus some cold meats and pickles. Oh and Crackers.

Making a list she thought she must run the gauntlet of the supermarket. It may take some time as they are already getting busy. The presents were already bought, so she put wrapping paper on her list.

That was always a happy time, I loved wrapping presents. Putting them under the tree ready for the little ones to come and open. I am looking forward to Sunday when all the children are coming round to decorate the house for Christmas. I have all the Christmas decorations ready and I have the feeling that we will be using them all. Everything that we stored in the loft. Decorations from many years ago.

You know I hate you taking tablets, putting strange substances into your body. Always been the way with you, something not right? Here is a tablet. Take the easy way out as you always did.

Sunday 19th December.

Early start for me today. I went to the stables early and got everything ready for Nicholas to go out in his paddock and then come in again when it is about to get dark. Poor horses spend so long in their stables at this time of the year, but as long as they have enough to eat and are warm and comfortable they will be alright.

I know the children are coming over for lunch and then we will get the decorations up. One of the girls at the yard is going to bring Nicholas in for me today so I will not have to go back, which means I can have a glass or two of wine. I hope I can drink with these tablets. I had better read the blurb in the box. Actually, I don't care. I am going to have a drink.

Although, I have my appointment tomorrow with the counsellor, so I had better not drink too much. I really don't want to go to see her with a hangover.

Oh Harry, the old house looks really festive. We have used every decoration that I ever bought. They are everywhere. There are plastic Christmas trees in each room and Eric bought a huge real one to have in the big lounge. All the presents will be under that and I have set the open fire to light so we can have a really traditional Christmas afternoon. There is tinsel hanging from every light-fitting. Every bauble is hanging somewhere. I am hard-pushed to see the walls. It looks gorgeous.

Every room looks like Santa's grotto. There are high level ones and, from Dee and Zoe, low level ones. Only a few days to go now Harry. The children as getting so excited. I love to see them having so much fun.

It warms my heart and goes some way to banishing the black blanket. I have so much love for these people, the big adult ones and the little ones.

How could I ever think of leaving them? How could you Harry? Just something else you are missing. This is the first Christmas without you. I have to make it a good one, one to remember and look back, with joy, not sadness. I just wish I could feel it whole heartedly. But it is there in the back ground, the terrible sadness, the deep dark oppression. Put on a happy face, wear it like a mask. Don't inflict this on anyone else, they don't deserve it.

'Will Grandpa come home for Christmas?' Zoe asked.

Paula smiled and told her that he was really sorry but he needed to spend Christmas in Heaven. She looked sad for a moment and then said. 'Well if he is needed there then we can do without him.' She rushed off to put some more baubles on the tree. Why can't I live in the moment like that Harry?

Perhaps I should learn a lesson from the little one.

161

Monday 20th December.

It's the day for my first counselling session. I have the appointment at 11 o'clock. It's in a private house which is better I think, than an office. But as I am parked up outside I am hesitant to go in. The time is ticking and I have been sitting here for twenty minutes. I was early just so I could make sure I knew where to go but perhaps I would have been better to arrive just in time and not have time to sit and over-think everything.

Shall I just drive away? But like an automaton I get out of the car and head for the front door.

I don't know what I expected. Well I did, because she sounded so efficient on the phone. I expected a tall well-dressed woman with short hair looking business like. It had made me nervous. But the lady who opened the door and greeted me was nothing like that. Tall, yes but also very round, and she wore a long flowery dress which fitted to her ample shape. She wore a long sleeveless coat over this and had so many strings of beads round her neck I thought she may topple at any minute. Big dangly ear rings, a shock of frizzy white hair, rosy red cheeks and bright red lipstick. I took to her immediately. Such a friendly face.

She smiled and said, 'Hello Paula, I am Davina. Do come in out of the cold, this way in my cosy room,'

We went into a small room that had two comfortable chairs. I sat down and she brought me a cup of coffee and put it on the table beside the chair. There was an open box of tissues on that table as well. Then I started to talk. And I didn't stop talking. She didn't stop me either, she just let me ramble on. She did take notes and after a while she clarified a few of the things I had said. She didn't offer advice as I had expected she just let me ramble on and put in encouraging comments every now and again. About how I felt about this situation and what did that make me feel like? I talked about you most of the time Harry, how much I missed you but also how much of me you had crushed.

'So, now you feel that life without Harry is more difficult that you had imagined it would be? That making decisions for yourself is becoming oppressive and you are starting to question the steps you have already taken?'

'Yes I feel that I have got so far but now I am not sure if I am doing the right thing.'

'Only you can know what is right for you. Harry is not here now to please or displease. You feel his disapproval, but what can he do to make it better for you or worse? I think you feel that your partnership was a bit one sided, that you felt that you gave more of yourself to the marriage than Harry did. Breaking that hold can be very hard. But you don't need to look to him for approval any more. You are grieving for him but he has gone and you still have a life to still live.'

'Which is exactly how I feel and have done all this time. Perhaps I should have given myself more time before I started making these big life changing decisions. I always used to say that nothing is forever, but now I feel that I am going to feel useless forever. Yes, I am questioning the moves I have made and I wonder if they were just a jerk reaction, a breaking free. If they are really what I want and just not what Harry would have wanted.'

'Well, nothing you have done so far is irreversible. You have bought the bungalow but you could always sell it. You have accepted an offer on your house but you could pull out. You can unmake the moves you have made, if that is really what you want. You have to put yourself first now Paula. You have no-one to answer to.'

'I know, and that is what is so frightening.'

'I am not going to tell you to pull out of the sale; I am not going to tell you to go ahead. What I hope to be able to do is give you the strength to make the decision for yourself, and let you know that whichever decision you make is right for you.'

I came out feeling, much better about everything already, having someone who is not involved to tell all my worries to, being able to unload. I couldn't tell the girls, I can't tell you. But I can talk it all through with Davina.

I will see her again after Christmas and she has booked me in for weekly sessions during January and February.

I am just going to enjoy Christmas, and not think about it at all until after I have seen her again. Nothing is going to need to be finalised before then and nothing is forever, things are all slowing down now anyway. I'm not saying that Christmas without you will be a blast Harry and I am going to miss you so much. But I realise that I am going to have to do this so many more times, this is just the first.

Christmas was always a time you enjoyed, the parties, the family, it was as if I was not enough for you that you had to fill our lives with all these other people. You tried to do that at other times as well but at least I managed to confine it to that one season. I didn't like you being able to enjoy the company of others, and having conversations with them that I didn't know about. Or be able to guide the conversation, to stop you from learning from those women. I didn't want that. The marriage we had suited me very well. I had to let you have Christmas but I wanted you to be home for me the rest of the time.

Friday 24th December.

I'm not going to think too much about anything right now. I am going to discipline myself to just get on with Christmas. Make it enjoyable for all of us. I have arranged a Christmas morning ride. I will have plenty of time as I am not going to have to try and cook dinner.

We would have been pottering around in the kitchen all morning you doing the cooking and me as your sous chef. Peeling the potatoes, preparing the vegetables and sometimes you would let me make the stuffing. Only if it was a simple one.

But tomorrow we are going out to lunch and coming back here for tea. I do have to make sure there are enough beds ready for everyone that is my job for the day.

Mrs. M, bless her is coming in to give me a hand and a quick spruce up, although she can't do much with all those decorations hanging everywhere. I have a present for her to take home to open tomorrow. Some nice perfume. I hope she likes it. I did ask if she would like to come over for afternoon tea, but she is going to her sister's house.

Tonight, I will sit alone and watch some silly movies on the TV. I didn't expect anyone to ring me this evening, so was a bit shaken when the phone rang. It was Brenda. She and Robert have been friends of ours for a long time. And I have to say that she is one of the few

165

who has kept in touch since you died. I have been invited to their New Year's party. We often went to that, it was always a big deal and Brenda works really hard to make it a good do.

I was a bit surprised but thanked her and said I would be happy to come along.

Well, that's nice. Something else to look forward to. Many of our friends will be there and it will be nice to catch up. When I said that they had all disappeared into the mist I do have to remember that I didn't actually keep in touch with them either. I feel a bit guilty about that now, blaming all of them for leaving me alone with my grief but thinking about it perhaps they were giving me time to heal. Or something like that.

But yes, I will go to this one. I have booked a taxi to come home so I can have a drink or two. Not intending to get drunk but one must toast the New Year in with a drop of champagne.

Robert is coming to fetch me on his round to get Joy and Michael. I haven't seen them for a while either. Yes, Christmas is perking up. I'm just sorry that you are not here to enjoy it with me, my love.

Well I'm not. I have already told you I don't want you going out. But if you must then you go alone. I certainly won't be coming with you. See how you get on at this do without me to tell you who you can talk to and supervise what you say.

Saturday 25th December Christmas Day

Our first Christmas apart, Harry. You would have got up and brought me a cup of tea and a mince pie in bed. We would have sat together and watched a bit of TV in the bedroom drinking and eating.

Then I would have had a leisurely bath and you would have brought me a Bucks Fizz. Having got dressed and had a proper breakfast it would be "Action Stations" to get the meal ready. Usually the bird would have been cooking slowly through the night. You were a dab hand at setting the timer on the cooker. I can't do that and can't be bothered to learn how to do it now.

Paula spent a few minutes preparing herself for the day ahead. It was going to be a very different Christmas this year, not just that Harry was not there but having decided earlier in the year to arrange lunch out she didn't know how it would pan out. Will they be able to make a success of it or would it all fall flat?

Right, enough of this thinking Paula told herself sternly. It was time to get a move on. Put on the cheery face and get this over with. She was really not looking forward to it. Not one bit. But with the painted on smile she prepared herself to endure the day.

Ride over, horse sorted. He had an extra carrot today. He seemed happy enough. Trish said she would do the afternoon shift and bring him in for his tea.

Paula was home now, having had a very enjoyable Christmas ride with the horses all decorated in tinsel. Time for that long hot bath, and then the Bucks fizz. She put some music on loud so she could hear it upstairs. She had plenty of time so she sorted through the Christmas CDs and chose the brightest one to dance about to.

She sang all the songs as well and thought that it was a good job no one was there to hear her. Singing was not a talent she possessed.

But she had read somewhere that singing produced endorphin's which help to cheer people up.

Sandi and John are picking me up about half past twelve. We can have a nice drink before we eat. I bet the little ones are buzzing. I have a small present to give them all at the pub but they will have to wait for the other presents till after lunch. Buck's Fizz and bath it is then. Then spend some time at the dressing table painting on my happy face.

All that went well Harry. There were three big families having lunch at the pub and it was like having a party. I really enjoyed it even though I had not been looking forward to it. We raised a glass to you, my darling. Happy Christmas.

The whole family went back to the house to play some board games, but first a walk to let the lunch go down. Eric and John's parents were going to pay a visit as well. This year they had both been to lunch with other members of their families. It is a lovely day with a weak sun trying to come through. It's not going to be a white Christmas, no snow was forecast. Paula had already lit the fire before they went out so the lounge would be nice and warm and the fire just needed stoking up a bit when they got back. Although with the heating going full blast the whole house was warm. With all that lot there would be thirteen to cater for at tea time.

A bit of a squash even in that big room. Paula, looked at her extended family and had a moment of pure grief

168

and self-hatred. The only one here who was not coupled with any one. No Husband, just that emptiness.

'Presents!' The kids all yell at once. Happy times, paper flying all around. Thank-you kisses exchanged and then they settle to game playing and normal Christmas squabbles.

I sit back and watch for a while and feeling quite detached as there is that bid something missing. You my darling. You should be here. Oh well, that will never happen again.

It was after the little children had gone to bed, and when Daniel and Rachel are settled with their new games that the adults really started talking about how much they missed Harry. Eric started with telling us how much has changed at work without you there. That actually they have more autonomy and can make changes in line with new trends a bit quicker. Eric and John have taken joint responsibility for running the business and everyone is pleased with the latest figures. Paula had been very hands off but the boys said they would love it if she was to come to some of the meetings.

'Will I be able to keep up with the new structure?' she asked them.

'We can bring you up to speed with it all, it's not much different but we could do with some new computer aids and stuff like that and would like you to okay it,' John said.

I said that would be alright if they really want me to but I can trust them to do the right thing for the business as a whole and didn't want to interfere.

I think Harry they just need the confidence to get on with it without having to refer to you every time they want to make a change. I feel that is exactly what I need as well. It struck me like a bolt of lightning that my depression and panic was all about having the confidence to go it alone. How strange that we should all feel the same. It just shows how much we all relied on you, never making a move in any direction without asking you if we were right. Did we put too much pressure on you, all of us? Or did you remove the pressure from us?

Did you take control of our lives in and out of work? I know I let you take control of my life and I have run amuck doing things I thought you would not like me to do, just to spite you. What I now have to decide is if those things are actually right for me or just a reaction against you?

Sandi said she was surprised that although she was grieving at the loss of you and your early demise she wasn't missing you so much as she thought she would. Molly felt the same, but maybe that was because they did not see you every day since they were married. Eric, John and I saw more of you than the girls did, in fact.

So we would miss you more, day to day. We didn't get maudlin, it was direct, honest talking. We all raised another glass to you Harry, and called it a night.

Sunday 26ᵗʰ December Boxing Day

Up and out to Nicholas, no riding today as I still have a house full. Home in time for breakfast. They are all staying for lunch as well. John agreed with me that the cold meats with pickles are even better than the Christmas dinner.

We laid it all out buffet style so people could just help themselves. So we spent the day nibbling, playing, watching TV, and just generally lazing about. A very nice way to spend a cold winter Sunday. When it was time for me to go back to Nicholas the families all packed up and went home. I came home to an empty house but I can't expect them to keep me company for ever.

It's alright I have plenty to do. New books to read, some knitting I have started and there is always a good film to watch. I can go riding tomorrow, weather permitting. All the girls will be at the stable yard as it is a holiday because of Boxing Day being on a Sunday. There are quite a few of us planning to go out so it should be a good ride. I am looking forward to it.

Then on Tuesday when the shops open again I will go and buy a new party outfit, for New Year's Eve.

That has always been a dressy occasion, and I intend to dress up for it. I'm going to have my hair done as well. It is growing quite well, not as long as I would like but at least I have a style to it now. I have stayed with the grey colour and lightened even more. I love not having to touch up roots to keep it blonde as you liked it.

In fact, I think I am going to be like my Mum and be white by the time I am sixty. You had lovely steel grey hair already when you died didn't you? I loved that colour on you. When you got a tanned face it looked

171

really impressive. I used to look at you and see other women watching you and think to myself. Look all you like but he is mine. Huh! Now I know you were not mine exclusively.

I still expect a knock on the door and some other woman to be standing there with tears in her eyes saying that you were the love of her life. But I may be maligning you. Maybe Sharon was the only other one. She will be married soon, less than a year since you died. How much did she love you? Poor Harry.

Don't start feeling sorry for me Paula. Watching her go her own way and deciding to let you go. I am fine thank you very much. I know my influence over you has declined and you are breaking all my rules. For all the good it will do you.

Friday 31st December.

It's party time. Paula is wearing a new dress and the fox fur stole Harry bought her was around her shoulders for warmth until she got into Brenda's house, although Robert's car should be nice and warm anyway, as he is picking Joy and Michael up first.

I have had my hair done and I must say it looks good. I feel fantastic in my new dress and shoes. It shows my new slim-line figure off to a treat but I am not flashing too much flesh. Too old for all that, leave it to the youngsters. Red, a nice bright warm colour. And I have my Ruby necklace and earrings on as well as that lovely bracelet you gave me last year. Cinderella off to the ball. Ahh! here is Robert, dressed in black tie and tuxedo. Good, I am not over-dressed.

'You didn't have to get out of the car Robert, I could just as easily come out to you.'

'Can't be letting my special guest come out without an escort, can I?' He said taking my arm after I have locked the door. I had the remote in my bag so I could close the gate after we left. And off we went. Joy and Michael greeted me as if they haven't seen me in years. Well it is nearly a year. I feel so wanted at last.

'Brenda all ready for this?' I ask.

'Of course, she always is. You know she starts making arrangements on the second of January, every year,' Robert laughed.

'Paula, how lovely to see you. My, haven't you lost weight? You look stunning. I am going to have to watch out that you don't go stealing all the limelight,' Brenda came over and gave me a big hug.

'Oops sorry, don't let me mess up your hair.' You know everyone here, don't you? Let's get you a glass of champagne.'

And so, the evening started. It was so nice to see all their friends again and Paula was having a great time.

I had some deep conversations regarding you with some of the ladies and reassured them that I was now feeling a lot better about your death and think I can cope now. Funnily enough, I found I could lie about this quite easily. I am not alright, but I wasn't about to admit it to these people. Anyway, they don't want to hear about my difficulties.

As I had suspected when I was talking with some of them, it was a case of them leaving me to grieve. I believed most of the ladies were genuinely concerned for me and wanted to get in touch but were leaving it until they thought I was ready. Some of the others however, I still don't trust. I think they believe that I will be going after their husbands now I am a widow. No way. Lovely as some of them are, they are not a patch on you my darling.

'Do you remember my little brother Peter? He is just home from South Africa. Home for good apparently, although I will believe that if he is still here this time next year,' Brenda said to me. I looked and saw the brightest blue eyes. Set in a tanned face bordered by still very blond hair.

'Peter, of course I remember you. How could I ever forget those eyes?'

'Bane of my life these eyes of mine. How are you Paula?'

'Much better for seeing you.'

'Likewise,' he said smiling brightly.

Oh, Harry he's flirting with me and I really want to flirt with him.

Well, that was it. The rest of the evening was spent with Peter. They talked, danced, drank, danced some more and continued to talk. He said that his wife had left him and that is why he has come home from South Africa.

They have no children and that was a great sadness for him but his wife never wanted any. He felt cheated that she had not mentioned this before they got married. He is looking for a house to buy locally as he has been transferred to this area with his work in the renewable power industry. She, his wife didn't want to come with him. She liked living in South Africa and was staying there.

'Oh, I'm so sorry,' Paula said.

'Don't be, I have many friends here and will do fine. How about you? How are you coping without Harry?'

'With difficulty,' she admitted.

So, the evening went on and then it was home time. The evening had rushed by. Paula realised that she had not thought about Harry very much at all, she had so much enjoyed chatting with Peter. She also felt good in herself that she had been able to reconnect with some of her friends. So in the taxi on the way home she found that the dread of returning to the empty house was not as keen as it had been before.

Don't get too used to it Paula. You are still my woman. I am watching you with that Peter I don't like the way this is all going. He will not be getting his feet under my table I can tell you that. Do you hear me? Paula?

Saturday 1ˢᵗ January

Peter called to see how I was. I had just got back from the stables and needed a bath, but we had a nice long conversation on the phone. Peter said that this is silly and instead of talking on the phone we should meet. I said why didn't he come around tonight? I would rustle up a meal of some kind. He said he would bring wine and would about seven pm be alright?

At five minutes to seven I pressed the remote to open the gate. And exactly at seven pm there was a knock on the door. There he stood a vision of male virility. Under his sheepskin coat he was wearing a blue silk shirt and jeans. He looked casual but smart. I had also opted for silk, but a dress.

The conversation continued. I can't believe how well we got on. No awkward silences, no pauses, we just clicked. He told me that he had always fancied me but I was already married to Harry so I was a no-go area. I was flattered but didn't really believe him.

After we had eaten we settled on the couch in the lounge where I had lit a fire. Cosy, on a chilly night. We seemed to be getting closer and closer, then Peter took matters into his own hands. He then leaned over and kissed me. Just a small peck on the lips but as I didn't immediately pull away he came back for another and this was much more a full on kiss. I felt it in the pit of my stomach.

I was breathless. Our lips fitted together so well and the kiss was reaching all parts of me with a zing. Tingling, I kissed him back and put my hand to his face

I looked into his intense blue eyes and saw desire. He moved his right hand to my neck and caressed my shoulder and back. Softly and gently at first.

Then his other hand came to my throat but moved down to my breasts. I felt a tightening that I haven't felt for a long time. I started undoing the buttons of his shirt so I could get to his chest, and soon as I touched his skin I felt so alive. It sent shivers down my spine glorious shivers. He undid my dress, and deftly undid my bra with one hand.

Hmm, I thought, he has done that a few times. But I didn't care. He started kissing my neck, chest and nipples, sucking and flicking his tongue over them, I was already gasping with desire for him but he didn't hurry. I let my fingers play over his back and chest and he did a little shake.

I pulled his shirt off and started to undo the belt of his jeans. He kicked off his shoes and carried on exploring my body. My dress came off and he covered me with kisses while removing my panties. I was feeling hot, wet and I was aching for him to enter me.

He wasn't ready to satisfy me yet. He stood up and removed his jeans pants and socks. I could see his desire from where I was sitting and tried to make a grab for it. Then he started with my feet. Kissing all the way up my legs until he reached my inner thigh. Slowly he caressed me there so close but so far. Then he entered me with a finger, rubbing me inside making me tighten with want. My breathing was coming in gasps and I wanted to scream at him to come in me.

'OH God,' I cried.

'No, just me,' he said gruffly.

I was pulsing with desire for him. I needed him in me and he knew I was ready for him. He came into me and the whole world exploded for me. I came. It was furious, it was earth shattering. It was life draining. I screamed as he pumped into me deeper and deeper filling up my whole body. I could feel him filling me with his desire and I could feel my climax flowing out of me. With an almighty yell he came in me and we collapsed in a heap.

We lay there for a while, and then he got up and stoked the fire, as it had died down a bit. I looked at his fit tanned body. I sat up so he could sit next to me.

'See I told you I had always fancied you,' he said with a smirk.

'It's just as well then, isn't it?' We pulled a throw over us and we went to sleep in wrapped in each other's arms. Right there on the couch, in our lounge Harry.

You whore. I knew it wouldn't take you long to become a mattress for any man that glanced at you. Do you have no respect for yourself? For me? You need to remember who you are my woman. You are just that, my woman.

Sunday 2nd January

'Can I see you again Paula?' Peter asked before he left.

'Yes, I think that would be acceptable.' I said trying a coy look.

'I don't want to monopolise you so how about next Saturday; the one coming I mean not next week?'

'I'll check my diary, Yep that seems to be free.' Not even bothering to pick up my diary.

'I'll come and pick you up and we will go out for a meal somewhere. Is 7 o'clock again alright?'

'Great, that will do nicely.' A quick kiss and he was gone.

It's still early and I need to get on. Nicholas first then home for a nice long soak in the bath. Do I tell the girls? Not everything, of course. Not how we made out on the couch. Not that we slept together, which is a nice way of putting what we actually did. Do I feel guilty?

A little bit. It's not a year since you went from me but did it make me happy? Oh yes, very. Feeling wanted, desired even but what if he doesn't turn up and was just using me for a quick one night romp. I can only wait and see. Do I want another man in my life? Not full time Harry.

I had you for all that time and that was enough for me. I don't want to give up my new-found independence. I wonder how Peter feels about it. I hope he liked what he got last night enough for a return visit, but I don't want him here all the time. No. But I did like the sex. I am a bit sore but feeling so good about myself. Just goes to show what making an effort gets you.

I wandered into the lounge and thought I had better clear up. I find my poor dress in a bundle on the floor. Along with my other clothing. Better take the dress to the cleaners. It looks a mess, but I can smell him on it.

Yes I can smell it on you as well, your sluttish wanton behaviour. You disgust me you whore. Although I did quite enjoy watching you, not to see you enjoy yourself that I found horrific. But watching people have sex. Yep I liked that.

Saturday 8th January

Paula was dressed and ready to go out for a meal. She had on a rather fetching new silk dress which she feels suited her age and complexion a treat. It was ten minutes to seven. Would Peter come? Or would he have changed his mind? Was she too easy and did he think she was a slut? Did he enjoy the sex they had last week? They had done some talking beforehand and got on really well.

179

But was that just his way to get me into the sack? I am a scribble of indecision. My mind is all over the place.

She has pressed the button and opened the gate so he could drive right in. If he didn't come she would feel such a fool.

Oh Harry, how you would laugh.

Check the make up again. Is it too much, should I wipe off the lipstick? I don't want to look desperate, but I want him to know I have made an effort for him. I feel like a teenager going on a first date. It never changes, does it? I am pacing around, picking up ornaments and shifting them somewhere else. All I can think about is, will he come?

A car just turned into the drive way. I waited. Then at exactly 7 o'clock he knocked on the door.

Big breath in and I went to answer it. Pasted on a big smile. He looked very smart in a rather nice and I guess, expensive suit.

'Ready?' Peter asked.

'Yes all ready, I answered taking his arm.

I am ready for this. Another step away from you Harry

Over the meal, we chatted away as if we were old friends. When we knew we would not be disturbed by the waiter for a while, Peter looked into my eyes and said;

'I really loved last week. You have a fantastic body and I had a wonderful time exploring it.'

I felt myself tightening up and getting goose bumps. Just the thought of maybe a repeat performance had me feeling as if I was about to have an orgasm right there at the table.

I couldn't talk properly for fear of giving myself away, my breath was coming in gasps. I was pulsing and could feel my body crying out for his touch. My nipples were hardening and he saw that, through my dress. I told him I needed to go to the loo and would be back in a tick.

In the ladies, I removed my bra, so he could see better, the tell-tale erect nipples. Then I went the whole hog and put my tights and knickers in my bag. All I was wearing at this point was my dress.

I went back to the table and sat down. He looked right into my eyes then down to my breasts.

'Not cold are you?'

'Why do you ask?'

'Well you are, how shall I put this? Standing out a bit,' he smirked at me.

'No, I am not cold; far from it, I am hot for you.'

'So, are up for a repeat?' He asked

Trying to sound in control I said

'Yes, I think so.'

Peter paid the bill and we went out to the car. As he opened the door for me he put his hand inside my coat and tenderly caressed my right breast. Flicking his finger over the outstanding nipple and giving it a squeeze.

Oh My. I nearly came there and then. Under the cover of my coat he leaned into me and pulled my skirt up a fraction. I parted my legs and let him know I wanted him. He felt that I had no knickers on and played with my clitoris and stroked my thighs.

We were in a very dark part of the car park and all the diners were inside. We felt safe enough. Well actually, I didn't care by this time anyway. I just wanted him inside me. I felt some fumbling and my skirt lift a bit more and then he was thrusting into me, right there leaning against his car, my coat wrapped round us. My skirt was round my waist, one of his hands clutching my bum the other squeezing my boobs.

His kisses fuelled the orgasm I had right there and then, He wasn't finished and thrust into me with such vigour I could feel him pulsing inside me so I wrapped a leg around him to bring him closer. He hoisted my other leg up round his waist and continued to ram into me making the car rock. *Oh Hell's fire*! I came again just as he did.

Once indoors we started again and had much more of the same until we were both spent. Then we had coffee and sat down, exhausted.

'Paula, I love being with you and making love to you. But…'

'You don't want a relationship,' I finished for him.
'That is absolutely fine, neither do I. My husband has not been dead a year yet and I certainly don't want to be tied down in any way. I love having sex with you though.'

'I prefer to think of it as making love,' he said.
I smiled at him and said, 'I prefer to think of it as fucking.'
Peter laughed and said, 'Too right, that's exactly what it is. And we fuck really well together.'

'So, if we are to continue fucking for a while but not have a relationship then we can just be Fuck Buddies.' I told him. 'I do need to be discreet though because I don't want my children to know.'

'Perhaps my coming here is not such a good idea then, maybe we should meet up somewhere else.'

'Be Mr. and Mrs. Smith in out of the way hotels?' I asked.

'It's a thought. We can always go away every now and then. Do a show in London and stay over.'

I laughed and said, 'What? Fuck in the stalls? Or were you thinking a bit more up market and a gallery fuck?'

We joked on like this a bit more and then went to bed. Before Peter left in the morning we arranged our next meet up.

Next Saturday we'll meet in the city and stay over. I told him that was good because at my age I needed a week to get over him.

Oh Harry, I feel so young again. Our lovemaking was very much like that when we were young and first in love. I don't love Peter, he doesn't love me but for now we suit for sex romps and that is good enough for me.

At least you will take your disgusting sluttish behaviour out of my house. Go sneaking around in pay by the hour hotels and screw your lover there. I find all this very distasteful Paula. You have not long been widowed, and you are acting like a wanton hussy.

Tuesday 18th January

My next appointment with Davina. And yes Harry, I did tell her everything, including how good the sex was. I also told her that I am going ahead with the sale of this house and moving into the bungalow. She said that already I seemed to have gained confidence in myself and did I think it was because someone had singled me out as special to them?

I said that I thought that may have something to do with it, and re-connection with some old friends. Lunch, with Brenda and Joy for instance. I don't go out much in the evenings most of my socialising seems to be during the day. Except for the weekly 'therapy' sessions with Peter, they go on all night long.

Davina told me that she thought for now I didn't really need her but I wanted to continue the sessions for a while. I really don't feel strong enough to go alone yet. What I really need is a point in the right direction and to let you go. That is hard, Harry, but I must.

Thursday 20th January.

I just received a phone call from the estate agents. The people who want to buy this house now have a sale on theirs. It seems all is now go. I asked when they thought they could complete on the sale and she said it would be sometime around the end of March or very early April. A long while she said but their buyers have not secured a mortgage yet. That always makes the process longer.

I told her that would be fine with me as I still have some work to do on the bungalow and more furniture to buy. The carpets are going down soon because the decorator has finished and I just want to make sure the paint is really dry.

Then I can start filling it up. I know the kitchen is ready to go so I can start putting the new things I have bought in there. The bathrooms both have flooring down and I can stock the cupboards in those as well. When I leave here Harry I will leave with one small overnight bag as everything else will already be in the bungalow.

I still have some sad moments when I really miss you. But I am slowly learning to live my life and not have you constantly in my thoughts. I have some routines now that I like to keep to. I go to the horse at about 7 o'clock each morning to put him out if I am not riding, do his stables and make everything ready for him to come in for the night.

Then I come home to shower and get ready for my day. I might go out then and have lunch with someone, see the girls, stay in and do some hobbies. All my time. All for me. I fill my days and usually have my evenings free. Now I find I don't really get lonely in the evenings Harry. I am used to spending them alone.

You would either be out, at work, or asleep. Apart from the nights I spend with Peter I like to have time for lolling in front of the television or listening to music while I knit or paint.

I have even started making some of my own clothes. I got the old sewing machine down from the loft at Christmas time and have set it up in your study. That is now my hobby room. Molly took your desk and I have set up another old table I found in the barn. I will be moving all my craft stuff to the bungalow when my hobby room there is sorted and carpeted.

I phoned Mr Fraser and informed him about the house sale. Life goes on Harry and I find that without you my life is fuller and much more fulfilling. It makes me sad that we missed all this but then again, I don't think you did miss it did you? Your life seems to have been much more active than I gave credit for.

And Sharon. Well she gets married at the end of this month. She is moving away so I will have that house empty. What should I do about that? Keep it and get another tenant? Maybe I should try and buy some more houses and rent them out and then the grandchildren could have them when they come of age. I will ask Mr Fraser about that. There are bound to be some pitfalls but it is worth a thought. Yes, next time I have an evening spare I will have a look online and see what is available.

I also talk on line with some of my old friends who don't live around this area any more like Jenny in Greece. That can fill an evening.

I still sit and read sometimes as I used to do while you slept the evening away. I always thought it was funny how you would wake if I left the room and wanted to know where I was going. It was as if you felt my presence leaving the room. Even if I was just going to the loo, you would follow if I was more than a couple of minutes.

At first I found it endearing, but it got really annoying towards the end. I would just sit there even if I wanted to go and do something else.

See how you filled my life? No wonder I still miss you.

I will be going soon Paula, I have places to visit and things to do. You seem to be getting on fine without me and I'm not sure I want to watch any more.

Tuesday 1st February

When Paula took the Christmas decorations down she threw them all away. Every Christmas memory went with them. Life starts anew. She had made the decision to move into the bungalow at the latest by the end of March, even if the house sale isn't completed by then. That would give her time to get the house clearance people in and get it all empty for when the new owners take over.

She spent most of the morning phoning to arrange for her new furniture to be delivered to the bungalow, now that the carpets were down and the painting all dry.

I have two months and there is a lot to do. Molly and Sandi are coming over to help me get all the small items there as they have cars that can carry it all.

'Of course, you could just hire a van, Mum,' Molly told me.

'Yes, I suppose I could but then everything would be there and I still don't have places to put everything. I can fill the kitchen and the bathrooms but wardrobes and such like are yet to be delivered. The curtain people are coming today to put the curtains up and the first of the furniture will be arriving on Monday. The only other room that is ready is the hobby room. I have the router and phone line going in there so can set up the computer space. Sewing machine, art and writing gear can come as well, but the ornaments I want to take will have to wait until I have the lounge furniture in.'

'What clothes are you taking with you?'

'Not much right now, as I still have two months before I want to move.'

'Oh, did you hear that Brenda's brother is home from South Africa?' Sandi asked.

'Really? I thought he was married and settled there.' I said innocently. 'Actually I did know I met up with him at their New Year's Eve party,' I giggled.

'Oh Mum,' They chorused.

'Yes, apparently, he has split from his wife.'

'Well, he always had the hots for you,' Sandi said.

'What, little Peter?' I said.

'Not so little now, he looks really good for his age. In fact if I wasn't so happily married to Eric I would flirt with him.'

'MOLLY,' Paula said, 'But I do agree, he is a bit of a looker.'

'Perhaps we had better get loaded up and stop this conversation, before we all get into trouble. You naughty girl Mum,' Sandi said.

Oh Harry, the web we weave.

So, it was that we took the first of my belongings to my new home. We spent a happy hour in the kitchen arranging where things would go. Then we went for a walk along the beach and stopped at a nice pub for a quick bite to eat. They seemed very friendly in there and it is walking distance from my house so I can pop in any time. On my own, or maybe with Peter.

I must hide the smile that thinking of him brings to my face.

'Well, we will give you a few days to sort out more stuff Mum, and take some more over. I really like the house and what you have done with it,' Molly said to me. 'I think you'll be happy there.'

'You've come to terms with me leaving our family home then?' I asked her.

'Oh God yes. Ages ago. I really like it and you will be closer to us to see the kids as well. It's on the route that Daniel takes from school, so you can expect him to pop in any time.'

'Oh, that will be fun, of course I am usually at the stables at school time so best if he lets me know.' I said thinking fast. Blimey, what if Peter was there and Daniel turned up out of the blue? How embarrassing would that be?

'Daniel is really getting on with his riding now, isn't he? How is John doing Sandi? I haven't seen him down there much.'

'No, He is having private lessons and says he won't ride with us until he is equally as good or better...'

'Ahh I see, Pride.'

Sandi laughed and we started discussing when to get another horse and what sort. It would have to suit Daniel and John, with Sandi and Molly in between.

'Well Daniel managed fine on Nicholas and he is fifteen hands high, so I should think something about that size would suit all of you.'

'Yeah, John's quite tall but he would be okay on something that size.'

'Well I know there is a stable coming up soon, so I can reserve it if you like and we can start looking for one.' I will, however need a bit of help with looking after them.'

'God, yes of course. We wouldn't expect you to do it all. In fact we can take some of the workload of Nicholas for you sometimes as well.'

Hmm, might be handy sometimes I thought to myself.

Wednesday 2nd February

The weather has closed in on us and it is really very cold. It's a good job I filled up the oil tank so I can have the heating on full blast. I can't go riding, it's too frosty and slippery. I have arranged lunch out with Brenda.

'Guess what!' she said as I met her at the cafe we go to.

'Do tell.'

'Peter has a girlfriend. He won't tell me who it is but I did some washing for him and his clothes smelt of perfume. It's definitely not his aftershave, a totally different smell.'

'But he hasn't been home long has he?' I asked her.

'Just before Christmas, he came home.'

'Wow, he didn't hang about, did he?'

'No, never been one to go slow, our Peter. What is that perfume you are wearing?'

'Number 5. I always wear it.'

'Oh, it's the same smell. So at least I know she has good taste.'

'Well if she is with your Peter, it goes without saying.'

'Oh silly girl.'

'What are you eating? Is Joy meeting us today?' I said to get off the subject.

'Mm. Yes she will be a bit late. Perhaps it's her.'

'Her what?'

'That Peter is seeing.'

'Well maybe, but Joy? Is she into extra martial activity?'

'Perhaps not.'

'Well, I am going to have that rather nice looking tuna steak with a salad.'

When Joy finally joined us Brenda went straight into the story of Peter's girl-friend.

Joy said that the only one of us that was free was in fact me. I felt myself blushing but I think I managed to explain it away as being, 'time of life. Hot Flushes and such like.

'Oh! You poor dear,' Brenda said.' I do know how you feel. I'm a martyr to it myself.'

I stayed in town when we had finished our lunch and went to a chemist. There I tried several perfumes and found one I liked that didn't smell anything like Number 5. I will wear that whenever I am with Peter and only then.

Oh, dear it would be so easy to be able to share but I can't, not yet, and it may all be over by the time I am ready do that.

Monday 14th February

What is wrong with me? I can't stop crying. I have been sorting out some of the old photos. I started by chucking away all the ones with no people in them. I suppose the scenery was beautiful enough to take a photo but I can't even remember where these places were. I have kept some by as they would be nice to copy to make paintings of. The rest can go. Of the ones with people in I have kept those that have you in Harry.

You were so handsome in youth and in your older age. So good looking. I am especially missing you today as it is the first Valentines without you. I always got a huge bouquet of flowers from you, a card and often a little gift. I in turn would buy you some books and some of that dark chocolate you liked so much. We would have a lovely cosy meal at home with candles on the table, and a bottle of champagne.

Today I am sitting here sorting these photos and crying. Things were going so well. House bought, house sold. Moving organised.

I have built a social life and I am an independent woman who thought I could cope but looking at our life together in pictures I am in pieces. Each time I see your smiling face it's like the knife in my heart is twisted a bit further. It hurts, physically hurts.

I know now what people mean when they speak of the pain of loss. There you are, when the children were little. Christmas time, holidays, dinner dances when we were dressed up, all in flat pieces of paper. But the memories they bring.

Oh Harry, you were too young to die, I scream through my tears. I would go back to being the woman I was if it only meant that I could have you back with me. The black hole in my heart is getting bigger and has become a chasm in my soul. I need your touch, I need you to touch me, my skin yearns for your caress.

I keep having visions of you on the day I came to see your body. Even though I couldn't see all your face I still had the feeling that you were just asleep and would wake and hold me. I feel the pull of your tree. I was there yesterday,

I sit there and put my head beside the broken bark where the rest of the buck shot landed.

I can just about still feel you there, but it is not a pleasant feeling anymore, it's rather ominous and malevolent. Do you blame me for your death Harry? I feel as if you are angry with me. Is that because I didn't follow you, didn't come with you into death? Should I follow you, Is that what you want? Right now, I feel as if I don't belong here.

I wander round the house, starting jobs, leaving the photos and not able to finish anything I start. Then a wave hits me and the pain washes over me making me want to cry again. Then I sit and let the black cloak of despair wrap itself around me again and all I want to do is be with you. The ugly black feelings creep up on me. Harry, I can't do this alone. I need you here.

Peter will never replace you in my life, in my heart, and in my soul. I just need your touch, I need to smell you again, hear your voice, caress your face and bury my own face in your hair and breathe you in. My body aches to hold you and my soul screams for you. Oh, Harry you were too young to die.

It's so surreal, I still can't believe that I will never see you again, hold your hand, feel your morning goodbye kiss on the top of my head. Hear you drive away to work and listen for your car and you coming home walking in saying 'How's my favourite blonde?'

We would spend many an evening in companionable silence. Was it companionable? Or did we waste all those years? Was it a show we put on of being a loving couple? We were at first, we were inseparable.

Now we are separated by time, space and death. Till death do us part, but we should have had another thirty years at least Harry. But now I am here and you are?where are you Harry? Where are you now when I need you?

I must be brave. Davina says it's alright to cry, but like this? With this gut wrenching hurt, this pain in the chasm of my chest where my heart used to be. My broken heart, my shattered soul. I rock backwards and forwards keening in my grief. In my lament. I am not able to function, to think of anything, but how very sad I am, how I miss you.

Come on woman, you know you are breaking Harry's law. The crying is not attractive and to be brutally honest if you are to carry on being like this I really don't want you near me. You have been busy telling me you have a life to live and you must go on without me. I am beginning to feel that it was for the best that I left you. I suppose I would have faced this if you had found out about Sharon before I died. On reflection I am quite glad I don't have to be there to comfort and calm you. I would have had trouble keeping my temper from showing. I suppose I did go out of my way to make you so dependent on me I don't know I why did that but just knew I had to have you with me always and the more complacent and tubby you got the better I liked it.

Tuesday 15th February

I get up and go about my business, but there is no joy in it for me. The sadness carries on. There is light out there but I don't really want to see it. I want to hide under my black cloak of despair. Like an automaton, I go about my day to day life, chat to people, and even crack a laugh every now and then. I don't think people know what I am going through.

But why now? Ten months after you have died. Have I been denying my grief? Is this the way it will always be? Do I have to live with this pain for the rest of my life?

If so Harry I may as well follow you. I hear you calling to me and I am thinking I should come to you. I see no future without you. But I know I will carry on, I don't have the courage to actually do the deed and come to you. I have to finish this life; as long as it may be. I have to live my days alone. It is my fate.

Paula hated this feeling of depression that had descended on her again, she knew it was in her to shake it off.

The increase of the drugs were beginning to help and the doctor had told her she was still on quite a low dose. She was fearful that she would have to take them for the rest of her life. She knew that she could not join Harry and had even lost the feeling that he wanted her there with him. Did he ever want her? Well in the early days of course he did but as she got older and fatter he obviously didn't want to be near her.

But she supposed that each anniversary she would feel down. Yesterday being valentine's day which Harry had made a big deal of was just another of those anniversaries. Gird your loins, paint on the happy face, sing some songs and go about your daily business, she told herself.

Wednesday 1st March.
The doctor said that as he had increased the dosage of the anti-depressants and that she should start to feel a bit brighter soon. Paula was still full of questions about her own life. At the end of the month she was moving out of the house to her bungalow.

Will it be right for me? Will I feel happier? I thought moving out of this broken old house would be good for me and starting a new life. I have so much to look forward to and new things to try. I am not feeling it though. I just feel sad and, as my mum would say, down in the dumps. I still break down in tears for no apparent reason.

Most of the things she wanted to take with her were already at the bungalow and all she had here at the old house was enough to pack in one suitcase. She wandered around the rooms which although still furnished felt empty. Her new home was furnished and ready.

Why am I sad Harry? It is what I wanted. To break away from my old life and start a new one. Perhaps I should go now, why am I staying here?

The bungalow is ready and I have nothing to keep me here. I could just move in and leave this house empty for a few weeks. We have exchanged contracts so I do know it is sold. I don't have to stay. Yes, I will go. I will start my new life.

Yes, you go Paula, I feel that I am moving on as well, this house and all the memories are not holding me as tight as they did. When you go I think I will be heading off as well. Have your life. In a way I hope you enjoy it but there is a part of me that does not want to let you go. It is hard to realise that I have no control over you now.

When they first met and Harry had fallen head over heels in love with Paula, he knew he had to have her exclusively.

I could not trust the fact that you loved me and would stay faithful to me. I was first attracted by your lovely long blond hair. I reasoned that if I found it so attractive then so would other men. You see I had my reasons for keeping you tight to me. I was in fact jealous of your love for your horses. I wanted to be your world and that is what happened. But I didn't like it when I had you there. I wanted someone who would challenge me and you no longer did that. You complied with my every wish. You bored me, and I had to go and find excitement somewhere else. So go now and have your life. I will be here for a while yet but will leave eventually.

Sunday 5th March

The whole family is round here today for a last Sunday lunch in this kitchen. It should be a happy occasion. We decided on a roast for lunch with all the trimmings. Molly made the Yorkshire puddings, I never could get them right. It is a bit hotch-potch as I didn't have a complete set of cutlery or crockery any more.

I am going to sleep in the bungalow tonight Harry and when we have cleared up we will all leave together. I have packed my case and it is in the car.

So here we are, seated around the big table with an extra space for you. We toast to you and have our meal. It is surprisingly genial because the children are excited about the move. Rachel has told me that she was always nervous sleeping in this house, especially since you died. That will be why she often ended up in my bed when she stayed. She said she was alright in the tent camping but indoors she didn't like it. Were you watching over her Harry? She can be very sensitive.

'Well I hope the next family will be as happy here as we have been,' says Molly holding up her glass in a toast.

Were we happy here Harry? I'm not so sure I was. I seek happiness but it eludes me at the moment. Perhaps I shouldn't try so much. But today Harry I'm leaving you, finally. If you choose to stay here then that is your decision, but I am going.

'What will we do with all this stuff Mum? Sandi asked when we had washed up.

'We are going to smash it all and put it in the skip out there. It can go with all the other rubbish in this house that no one wants.'

'Can we do it?' Daniel asked.

'Of course you can.'

Yes that is about the last of the rubbish we lived with all these years Harry.

So out they all trooped with arms full of crockery and stuff. Paula had already set up some steps for the little ones to stand on by the skip and they had a brilliant time throwing everything in there. The noise is tremendous. Smashing, tinkling and laughing. Paula laughed to see how much fun the children were having and she found that she was smiling a genuinely happy smile. A last look around and they all leave. Paula locked the door lock and realised that she may never do that again. She will open it on the completion day to greet the new owners but she won't ever lock it up again.

'See you at your new house then Grandma,' Daniel calls as he gets in to Eric's car.

Yes, we are prolonging the day by having the first Sunday tea at my new house.

Paula had been busy in her new kitchen making cakes, scones and jam filled tarts. She would open another bottle of wine and the children had some cola, for a treat.

Not too much because she worried they may have a sugar rush. But it was a celebration.

I arrive at the bungalow first which I think is a bit strange as they all left before me. I unlock the door and go in. Fill the kettle and set the tea table. Then they all arrive just as I was opening a bottle of white wine that had been cooling in the fridge.

'We thought you should have a few minutes alone' Sandi told me. 'To get the feel before we all descended on you.'

'Go and explore then children and tell me what you think,' I say.

Eric and John went with them, neither of them have seen the finished place.

'I love your garden Mum,' Molly said. 'It will be lovely when all those shrubs establish.'

'I hope so,' Paula answered. 'I have opted for bee friendly plants.'

….

Paula said she was still full from lunch and as there was so much to eat for their Sunday tea she said. 'We could always go for a quick walk down the beach before tea to make a bit of space for it. Or you will all be taking so much home with you.'

And that is what they all did but they were only out for half an hour as it was really very chilly down by the sea with an easterly wind which meant it came right at them, off the sea. Paula told them she was just popping off to see to Nicholas but would be back very soon. Daniel opted to go with her. Daniel brought him in from his paddock and they got him settled for the night with his tea in his nice warm stable and then back to Paula's first night in her new house.

My house Harry. Not ours. Mine.
When we had cleared up after tea and the family had all gone home I looked about me. I felt unsettled. It was all so new. Shall I sit quietly and read? Shall I watch the television? Or have the radio on?

I don't feel you at all Harry. You stayed at the house. Did you love that house more than you did me? Or are you in a huff because I dared to move out of it? I didn't want you to come here, but I am a bit miffed that you haven't. How contrary of me.
So I had a little weep. I felt so alone again.

Until, that is, a neighbour knocked on the door to say welcome to the neighbourhood. She didn't want to come in but had just brought some flowers. I was a bit suspicious that she would be a busybody but she seemed really nice and was someone I had not met before, her name was June.

She said she hoped I would be happy here and she was quite glad that all the work had finished. I said I hoped they had not been too disturbed by the builders.

She said that it had been a bit noisy some-times but that was to be expected.

'Everything is all done and dusted now though,' June said as she left.

Paula had to think where it was she had put those lovely new vases. \she found them eventually in one of the cupboards in her nice useful utility room.

She took her time arranging the flowers in the vase, something she had never bothered doing before. She used to just stick them in a vase and hope for the best, but now she was taking time to make them look nice.

Then she placed them in various positions around her big open plan room until she decided where she liked them best. Then having washed up the tea things, only the ones that would not fit in the dish washer, and tidied up she was at a bit of a loss. She could watch some television, or listen to some music. In the end she sat in her new reclining chair and read a book until it was an acceptable time to go to bed.

I don't want anything to do with that little box you are now going to call home Paula. You will regret leaving my house. After all the space you had and those big airy rooms. A gentleman's residence that house is and you have shown your true self by moving to a nasty little housing estate. Well what can one expect from one such as you? Never happy were you? You could never quite rise to the standards I expected. You had plenty to do there to keep any woman perfectly happy. But it was never enough, you wanted what you had been brought up with and I couldn't quite get that out of you. So you stay in your little box Paula, Don't expect me to come down to your level.

Monday 6th March

My new life began. I got up had a leisurely shower and then went to see Nicholas. As it was not raining I went for a ride with some of the other girls. It was quite jolly. In the afternoon, I went to the writers circle and introduced myself to them.

They all sit in a local cafe and do their own writing but have quiet chats at well. I felt I would get on well there.

I had a cake with my coffee. Back to put Nicholas to bed and home again.

In Paula's brand new fridge she had loads of healthy food and decided her new life in her new home would be much healthier, So she cooked herself a proper healthy meal of Salmon and green beans. Feeling suitably virtuous she sat down to enjoy a television series she had started watching. She knew she would not have watched a crime drama with Harry.

He got bored with them and was convinced he knew who had done it so would just turn it off. Now Paula could settle down to enjoy the entertainment.

Molly phoned to see how her first night had gone.

'Lovely, my bed is really comfortable and I don' have to wrap myself in two cardigans to get out of bed, It is lovely and warm in this little house.'

'I didn't disturb your program did I?'

'No you rang just as the credits were coming up. Yes I had a great night and I'm really going to like living here. I don't miss the house at all and if I want to go for a walk I can. Will you want me to pick Rachel up one night from school? Now that it is only a ten minute walk away.'

'Well, there you see I did have an ulterior motive for calling,' said Molly, with a chuckle. 'Rachel would love you to pick her up Wednesday and take her to dancing.

'Yes of course. So long as she doesn't mind going up to Nick after her dance class. I may just pop out and get her and Daniel some boots to keep in my tack room at the yard just for these times.'

'She told me to ask if the Shetlands would be there? I don't think she will be much help, she will just want to cuddle the ponies?'

'Ahh. I'm sure that will be fine. I'm not sure when I will be in but if you want to pop round any time you will have to take pot luck.'

Paula told Molly about the visiting neighbour and the little chat she had been able to have with June. Also about the flowers and they had a laugh about how long it had taken her to find just the right place for them. Paula said she would soon feel at home but at the moment it felt a bit like staying in a hotel.

'I think, can I go and make a cup of tea? Then I tell myself not to be so bloody stupid, of course I can, my teapot, and my kettle. I'll get used to it but still feels a bit strange.'

'I know how you feel Mum, I felt like that when Eric and I first moved in here. Just give yourself a virtual slap across the face and get on with it. Your house, your rules.'

The conversation went on for a while and then Molly said goodnight.

Sandi was next. 'You've been on the phone ages. I tried ringing earlier.'

Yes, Molly beat you to it, I can't help feeling she must have been poised to ring just as the credits came up on that murder mystery. Paula said laughing.

'Ha ha yes, I was poised as well, but got in second. Well, how is it?' So very much the same conversation came about with Sandi as Paula had just had with Molly. Sandi invited Paula round to family tea on Thursday.

'Lovely what time?'

203

'About six or is that Nick time? John says he will go and do him for you if you like.'

'I think you may be losing John to horses. He seems to have found a new hobby.'

'No we will have to find one like Nick that we can all ride, then he can enjoy it and so can I. I'm really looking forward to the next lesson,' Sandi said.

'There may well be a stable coming vacant soon so perhaps we had better start looking for another family horse.'

'John will be over the moon and so I think will Daniel. He is really coming on well isn't he? John says he is about ready to have some joint lessons again. He reckons he has caught up with us he really wants to get out now.'

'Well the weather is improving all the time so that will be lovely.'

By the time she had finished her conversation with Sandi, Paula thought it was about time to have her second night in her new house. She went to bed and slept peacefully.

Paula didn't feel the need to go back to the house. In fact, she just didn't want to go there at all. She would have to on last day of the month to hand over the keys to the new owners. That will be soon enough. Meanwhile she was busy getting her life together and beginning to feel that there is a light at the end of the tunnel regarding her depression. Is it the drugs or the changes that had done that she wondered?

But I don't care either way. I just want to feel better. I need to make my mark in this place. I have to get to know the neighbours. I wrote some cards out for the near neighbours, inviting them round to see the changes I had made to the bungalow. And, to introduce myself to them. I gave a time when I would be home and waited to see if there was a response.

Monday 13ᵗʰ March

It's the day I had invited neighbours round. From 2 o'clock on-wards, I have been through with the vacuum to make sure everywhere is still clean from the last time Mrs. M came in and then I put the radio on. I thought I would sit and read to keep busy in case none of them came around.

'Hello Paula,' said June as I answered the door to six lovely looking ladies. As they came in they told me where they lived in relation to my bungalow. I was busy making tea and handing out cake and we had a jolly time. Some of them knew that I had recently lost my husband and were very sympathetic. They told me of all the activities that happened in the area.

Where the Women's Institute met and when, the painting group also gather at the village hall. I will be having a full life that much is for certain.

Many of these ladies are a good bit older than me and have lived in this part of town for many years.

They told me about the people who used to live in my bungalow and that they were well liked. So these ones were June, Joyce, Nicola, Lesley, Hazel and Mary. They told me that they all met up for lunch at the pub down by the beach weekly and invited me to join them on Friday.

They were all interested to hear about Nicholas and asked me about my family and children and grandchildren. I was told all about theirs as well. It was a fun and enjoyable afternoon. I will be going to lunch with them on most Fridays it seems. Lunch with the convent girls, lunch with our old friends. Lunch with these new friends. I will not be using that lovely new kitchen very much.

Friday. 17th March

Lunch out with the ladies. I needed to ask again which grandchild belonged to each lady. They were amused but realised that they had bombarded me with a lot of information so were quite indulgent with me. We found that we had some friends in common and I recognised another of the ladies from Brenda's party. I think I am going to fit right in here very nicely. I have even joined the 'knit and chat' group.

Molly laughed and asked if the family would expect new jumpers for Christmas this year. All of a sudden life has got so busy that Paula didn't have time to miss Harry. In fact she noticed that she hadn't even thought about him for a few days.

Does this mean I am free of him at last? I am not talking to him anymore. He must have stayed at the house. Well I hope the new owners don't mind sharing their new home with him.

With Nicholas being so close now I find that I am able to ride more. I often go up to the stables as soon as it is light and ride then do my chores. Then I come home, get clean and go and do one of the other activities. I still see Peter and we have the most glorious sex, even here sometimes but more usually in a hotel. That will end one day but it is great while it goes on.

We are now searching for another horse to add to our family. Daniel is a good rider and is very keen to help out with looking after two of them. Molly and Sandi are enjoying their riding as well. I am looking forward to be going out for family rides.

My garden is beginning to look really nice with the warmer spring weather. When the garden designers planted it up I told them I wanted flowers all year if possible. They did a good job and I was watching the snowdrops, crocus, and other spring bulbs come and go while I was still coming over daily. Now I have moved in the daffodils are appearing and some of the shrubs are budding up. I love my bungalow. I feel really comfortable here and also feel so much happier.

After all the doubts, misgivings and indecision I know I made the right choice.

The only thing that hangs over me now is that I have to go back to the house and hand over the keys to the new owners. I am not looking forward to that one bit. I could let the estate agents do it or the solicitors, but I feel that I must make this one last gesture to Harry. To say a final goodbye.

Friday 31st March
So I am back at the house. The new owners are not expected for another hour. So I have plenty of time to say goodbye to you Harry. I wander down to the copse and sit by your tree. I look into the woods and still expect to see you emerge with a dead rabbit or two. I think of that

night. The night you died. A year ago now Harry. So much has happened in that year, I have lived through all the anniversaries and managed to get by.

I am living a completely different life and I love it. Busy and fulfilled.

With the selling of your boats and guns there is loads of cash for me to squander if I want. I have a whole new wardrobe and don't have to account to you for every penny I spend. I have a nice new little car, a nice new little bungalow, some new friends and some re-connections with old ones.

Your attempt to keep me here under the supervision of our daughters didn't quite work how I suspect you wanted it to. But that will be resolved with the sale of the house so they have the cash to pay the tax bill you landed them with.

The girls and I are still discussing what to do with the house you owned. To buy more and rent them? There is a tenant in there now and they are paying a proper rent. I am putting all that money into a trust fund for our grandchildren.

Mr Fraser got me in touch with a financial adviser and he has set that up for me. Yes, so much has happened. The year has flown by and here we are again.

You were drunk that night, more than usual. You had gone out with the gun. It was dark and I wondered how you would be able to find anything to shoot. I didn't hear any shots and began to worry about you. Where on earth had you got to? I was getting so worried that I had to go out and look for you. I searched all around the garden and then thought I could see something down by the copse.

That's where I found you. Sitting by the tree. I went over to you. The gun was lying on the ground beside you. You had always said they were best kept dry and I thought it would get wet if I left it there like that. I tried to wake you to get you indoors but you had drunk so much you just mumbled something incoherent and would not get up. I couldn't lift you and there was no one about to help me get you indoors. So I thought I would have to leave you there sitting by the tree. It was the best I could do for you. I tried to cover you up as much as I could so you would not get too drenched if it started to rain.

But what do I do with the gun? I could just take it indoors but I thought you would be angry if you thought you had lost it. I leaned it up against the tree. It slipped and fell again. So I leaned it up again and wrapped your arm around it to keep it up there. Did I realise it was pointing straight at one side of your head Harry? Did I notice that your thumb was rather close to the trigger guard? But it was at least staying propped up and hadn't fallen down again.

I didn't hear the shot until I was nearly back indoors.

I went in and shut the door. Then I took my coat off and went to bed.

Dear Reader

If you liked this book please visit my Amazon page and leave me a review
https://www.amazon.co.uk/Diana-Bettinson/e/B06W9KGM7N/ref=sr_ntt_srch_lnk_1?qid=1525090700&sr=8-1

Also you can visit my Facebook author page for more updates on my writing
https://www.facebook.com/Dbettinson/
On twitter https://twitter.com/dibett

You can also learn about my children's books

Mouseapilla.
A colouring book for younger children

Gari. The life story of a Mini Cooper.

Acknowledgements

I have so many people to thank who helped me with the production of this book.
Suzan Collins who produced the fantastic cover. Without her there would be no book. Claire Walker who proof read the first draft. Franky Sayer who gave me some useful advice on editing. And my lovely husband John who did the last proof read.

Printed in Great Britain
by Amazon